THE BREAD
OF THOSE EARLY YEARS

BOOKS BY HEINRICH BÖLL

Acquainted with the Night
Tomorrow and Yesterday
Billiards at Half-past Nine
The Clown
Absent Without Leave
18 Stories
Irish Journal
End of a Mission
Children Are Civilians, Too
And Where Were You, Adam?
The Train Was on Time
The Bread of Those Early Years
Group Portrait with Lady
The Lost Honour of Katharina Blum

THE BREAD
OF THOSE EARLY YEARS

Heinrich Böll

TRANSLATED FROM THE GERMAN BY
LEILA VENNEWITZ

Secker & Warburg
London

Originally published in German as
Das Brot der frühen Jahre
Copyright 1955, Kiepenheuer & Witsch, Cologne,
7th edition 1972, and Ullstein Verlag,
"Ullstein Buch Nr. 239," Frankfurt/M, 1972.

This translation first published in England 1976 by
Martin Secker & Warburg Limited
14 Carlisle Street, London W1V 6NN

SBN: 436 05450 7

Photoset and printed
in Great Britain by
REDWOOD BURN LIMITED
Trowbridge & Esher

124695

Translator's Acknowledgment

I am deeply indebted to my husband, William Vennewitz, for his assistance in this translation.

Leila Vennewitz
Vancouver, Canada

PART ONE

THE day Hedwig arrived was a Monday, and that Monday morning, before my landlady slipped my father's letter under the door, I wanted more than anything to pull the covers up over my face, the way I often used to do when I was still living at the apprentices' hostel. But out in the hall my landlady was calling: "There's a letter for you—from home!" And when she slipped the letter under the door and it slid snow-white into the grey shadow still filling my room, I jumped out of bed with a start, for instead of the usual round postmark I recognized the oval one of an express letter.

In all the seven years I had been living alone here in the city, Father, who hated telegrams, had sent me only two such express letters: the first telling me about Mother's death, the second about his accident, when he broke both legs—and this was the third. I tore it open and was relieved to read: "Don't

9

forget," wrote Father, "that Muller's daughter Hedwig, for whom you have found a room, is arriving today by train at 11:47 A.M. Do the right thing and pick her up, and remember to buy a few flowers and to be pleasant. Try to imagine the feelings of a girl like that: she's arriving alone in the city for the first time; she doesn't know the street, she doesn't know the district where she's going to live; everything seems strange, and the big station with all those crowds at midday will scare her. Bear in mind that she is twenty years old and is going to the city to become a teacher. A pity you can no longer keep up your regular Sunday visits to me—a pity. Affectionately, Father."

Later on I would often wonder how things would have turned out if I hadn't met Hedwig at the station: I would have stepped into another life, the way a person might step into another train by mistake, a life that, in those days, before I knew Hedwig, seemed tolerable enough. Anyway, that's what I called it when talking to myself; but the life which stood waiting for me like the train on the other side of the platform, the train one nearly took, I now live that life in my dreams, and I know that what seemed tolerable enough at the time would have turned into Hell: I see myself standing around in that life, I see myself smiling, hear myself talking, like a twin brother seen in a dream, the smiling, talking brother one has never had—the brother who, perhaps for a fraction of a second, was on the brink of being conceived before the seed carrying him perished.

At the time, I wondered why Father had sent this letter express, and I wasn't sure whether I would have time to meet Hedwig's train, for ever since I have been specializing in the repair and servicing of automatic washing machines my weekends and Mondays have been unpredictable. It is on Saturdays and Sundays, when the husbands are off from work, that they tinker with the washing machines because they want to investigate the quality and workings of these costly acquisitions, and I sit by the phone, waiting for calls that often summon me out to the suburbs. As soon as I enter those houses I can smell the scorched odour of burnt-out contacts and wires, or I am faced by machines belching soapsuds like in a cartoon, by crestfallen husbands, weeping wives who, of the few buttons they have to push, have forgotten to push one or have pushed one twice. Then I savour the nonchalance with which I open my tool bag, examine the damage with pursed lips, calmly manipulate switches, levers, and connections, and with a pleasant smile, while I am preparing the correct mix of detergent, explain all over again how the machine works, turn it on, and while I am washing my hands, politely listen to the amateurish shoptalk of the master of the house, who is happy to see his technical know-how taken seriously. Then when I ask for a signature to my work sheet, most people don't look at it too closely, and I stroll to my car and drive off to the next emergency.

A twelve-hour workday, even Sundays, and now and then a date with Wolf and Ulla at Café Joos; on

Sundays, evening Mass, where, after usually turning up late, I would anxiously try to gauge from the priest's gestures whether the Oblation had already begun; my sigh of relief when it hadn't, as I sank down wearily into the nearest pew, sometimes falling asleep and only waking up when the altar boy rang the bell for the Transubstantiation. There had been hours when I hated myself, my work, my hands.

That Monday morning I was tired; there were still six calls left over from Sunday, and I heard my landlady at the phone in the hall saying: "Yes, I'll give him the message." I sat down on the bed, smoked a cigarette, and thought of Father.

I could see him walking through town in the evening to post the letter at the station in time for the train that stopped at Knochta at 10 P.M.; I could see him walking across the square by the church, past Muller's house, along the narrow avenue with its stunted trees; how then, to take a shortcut, he unlocked the big school gate, walked through the dark gateway into the school yard, looked up the yellow rear wall of the school building at his Grade 11 classroom, passed the tree in the middle of the yard with its stench of urine from the janitor's dog, and I could see Father unlock the small gate that is opened each morning from five minutes to eight till eight for the commuting students who come rushing out of the station across the street, while Hohnscheid, the janitor, stands by the gate to make sure none of the students who live in town sneak through the commuters' gate. Like Alfred Gruhs, the stationmaster's son, who had to take the long and dreary route all around the block because he wasn't a commuter.

On summer evenings the sun burnishes the classroom windowpanes. During the last year I spent in Knochta, I often walked this way with Father in the evening when we took letters or parcels for Mother to the station in time to meet the train, coming from the opposite direction, that stopped at ten thirty in Brochen, where Mother was in hospital.

Usually Father returned home by the same shortcut through the school yard, since it meant a saving of four minutes and saved him the detour around that ugly block, and because he usually had a book or some papers for marking to pick up. The memory of those summer Sunday evenings inside the school gripped me in a kind of paralysis: grey dusk filled the corridors, a few lonely caps hung on the clothes-hooks outside the classrooms, the floor had been freshly oiled, the silvered bronze on the war memorial gleamed dully beside the large snow-white square where Hitler's portrait used to hang, and General Scharnhorst's collar shone scarlet outside the staff room.

I once tried to filch a blank, stamped report form that was lying on the staff-room table, but the paper was so impressively stiff and rustled so much when I tried to fold it and push it under my shirt that Father, who was standing at a bookshelf, turned around, snatched it angrily out of my hand, and threw it back on the table. He didn't try to smooth it out, nor did he scold me, but from then on I always had to wait

13

for him out in the corridor, alone with General Scharnhorst's scarlet collar and alone with the red of Iphigenia's lips, whose picture hung outside Grade 12, and I was left with only the grey gloom of the corridor and now and then a glance through the peephole into Grade 12. But the people only permitted a look into more grey gloom. Once I found an ace of hearts on the freshly oiled floor: the red was the same as that of Iphigenia's lips and Scharnhorst's collar; and mingled with the smell of the fresh oil was that of the school lunch. Outside the classrooms I could clearly see the rings made by the hot canisters on the linoleum, and this smell of soup, the thought of the canister that would stand outside our classroom on Monday morning, aroused my hunger, which the red from Scharnhorst's collar, the red of Iphigenia's lips, and the red of the ace of hearts could not satisfy.

On the way home I used to ask Father if he wouldn't look in at Fundahl's the baker, just to say good evening and, in passing, ask for a loaf or a left-over piece of the dark-grey cake whose layer of jam was as red as General Scharnhorst's collar. As we walked home through the silent dark streets, I would prompt Father with the entire dialogue he was to conduct with Fundahl—so as to make our visit appear accidental. I was amazed at my own gift for invention, and the closer we got to Fundahl's bakery, the more I urged him on and the better became the imaginary dialogue that Father was supposed to have with Fundahl. Father would shake his head vigorously because Fundahl's son was in his class and a poor student, but when we reached

14

Fundahl's house he would stop, hesitating. I knew how hard it was for him, but I persisted, and Father would invariably make one of those jerky turns like soldiers in a film comedy, step into the doorway, and ring Fundahl's bell. Sunday evening at ten, and every time the same wordless scene would follow: someone would open the door, although never Fundahl himself, and Father would be too embarrassed and too upset even to say good evening, and Fundahl's son, his daughter, or his wife, whoever happened to be standing in the doorway, would call back into the dark corridor: "Father, it's Mr Fendrich." And Father would wait in silence while I stood behind him, registering the smells of the Fundahls' dinner: a roast or braised bacon, and if the door to the basement happened to be open, I would smell the bread.

Then Fundahl would appear, go into the bakery, bring out a loaf, and, without wrapping it, hold it out to Father, and Father would take it without a word. The first time we had neither briefcase nor paper with us, and Father carried the bread home under his arm while I walked in silence beside him, observing his expression: it was always a serene, proud face, with never a trace of how hard it had been for him. When I tried to take the bread from him to carry it myself, he gently shook his head, and later, whenever we went to the station again on Sunday evenings to post a letter to Mother, I always made sure that we took a briefcase along. There followed months when I found myself on Tuesdays already looking forward to this extra loaf, until one Sunday Fundahl himself suddenly opened the door, and I knew at once from his face that we weren't going to get any bread: the large dark eyes were hard, the chin heavy as a statue's, and he scarcely moved his lips as he said: "I can only issue bread in exchange for ration coupons and on Sunday evenings not even then." He slammed the door in our faces, the same door that today is the entrance to his café, where the local jazz club holds its sessions. I had seen the scarlet poster: ecstatic Negroes with their lips pressed to the golden mouthpieces of their trumpets.

At the time, it took a few seconds for us to pull ourselves together and walk home, I with the empty briefcase, its leather as limp as an empty shopping bag. Father's face was the same as ever: proud and serene. He said: "I had to give his son an F yesterday."

I could hear my landlady in the kitchen grinding coffee, hear her gently admonishing her little girl— and I still wished I could go back to bed and pull the covers up over my head: I could still remember how nice it had been at the apprentices' hostel when I had been able to pull down the corners of my mouth and look so pathetic that the hostel superintendent, Chaplain Derichs, would have tea and a hot-water bottle sent up to the dormitory, and when the others had gone down to breakfast I would drop off to sleep again and not wake up till the cleaning woman arrived about eleven to tidy up the room. Her name was Mrs Wietzel, and I was very much afraid of her hard blue gaze, afraid of the righteousness of those strong hands, and while she smoothed the sheets and folded the blankets—avoiding my bed as if it were a leper's—she kept uttering the threat that to this day rings horribly in my ears: "You won't amount to anything, you won't," and her sympathy when Mother died and everyone was so kind to me—her sympathy was even worse. But when after Mother's death I again switched vocations and apprenticeships and spent days sitting around at the hostel until the chaplain found a new position for me—I peeled potatoes or stood around in the corridors holding a broom—by that time her sympathy had vanished again, and whenever she saw me she would utter her prophecy: "You won't amount to anything, you won't." I was afraid of her as of a screeching, pursuing bird, and I would escape to the kitchen, where I felt safe under Mrs Fechter's wing: I gave her a hand slicing cabbage to make sauerkraut and earned many an extra helping of pudding by grating the heads of cabbage on the big slicer, and I found comfort in the sweetness of the kitchenmaids' songs. Certain passages in these songs considered immoral by Mrs Fechter—such as "And he loved her in the great dark night"—had to be disguised by humming. But the pile of cabbages shrank quicker than I had expected, and there remained terrible days that I had to spend—broom in hand—under Mrs Wietzel's command. Then the chaplain found the job for me at Wickweber's, and after having been an apprentice bank clerk, sales clerk, and carpenter, I started at Wickweber's as an electrician.

The other day—seven years after my stay at the hostel—I saw Mrs Wietzel waiting for a tram, and I

17

stopped my car, got out, and offered her a lift into town. She accepted, but when I let her out in front of her building she said in a friendly manner: "Much obliged, I'm sure—but having a car doesn't mean that a person amounts to anything. . . ."

I did not pull the covers over my head, and I spared myself the decision as to whether Mrs Wietzel had turned out to be right, for whether I amounted to anything or not, it was all the same to me. I didn't care.

When my landlady arrived with my breakfast I was still sitting on the edge of the bed. I handed her Father's letter, and she read it while I poured myself some coffee and spread some jam on a slice of bread.

"Of course you'll go," she said, and she placed the letter on the tray next to the sugar bowl. "You'll be nice and invite her for lunch. Don't forget these young girls are usually hungrier than they'll admit."

She left the room to answer the phone, and I heard her say again: "Yes—yes, I'll give him the message— yes," and she came back and said: "A woman on Kurbel Street called, she was crying into the phone because she can't cope with her washing machine. She wants you to come at once."

"I can't," I said, "I have to take care of yesterday's calls first."

My landlady shrugged her shoulders and left. I had breakfast, washed, and thought about Muller's daughter, whom I didn't know at all. She was supposed to arrive in town last February, and I had chuckled over her father's letter, at his handwriting, familiar to me from his marking of the French tests I had failed.

"My daughter Hedwig," Muller had written, "will be moving to the city in February in order to commence her studies at the Teachers' Academy. I would appreciate it if you could assist me in finding a room for her. No doubt you will have no clear recollection of me: I am the Principal of Hoffman von Fallersleben School, where you too pursued your studies for a number of years"—thus euphemistically did he express the fact that at the age of sixteen, after having twice remained stuck in Grade 8, I left school as a failure. "Nevertheless," Muller went on, "perhaps you do indeed remember me, and I trust that my request will not overly inconvenience you. The room for my daughter should not be too elaborate, nor should it be unattractive; if possible not too far from the Teachers' Academy, yet—if this can at all be arranged—not in a predominantly working-class district, and furthermore I take the liberty of emphasizing that it is essential that the rent be reasonable."

As I read this letter, Muller turned into an entirely different person from the one I remembered: I remembered him as being easygoing and forgetful, a bit sloppy in some ways; but now the image of a pedant and penny pincher emerged which did not fit my recollection of him.

The word "reasonable" was enough to make me hate him, a man whom I by no means remembered as being hateful, or I hate the word "reasonable". My father can also tell tales about the times when a pound of butter cost one mark, a furnished room and breakfast ten marks, about times when you could take a girl dancing with thirty pfennigs in your pocket, and in the context of those stories the word "reasonable" is always uttered with a reproachful undertone, as if the person who is being told about it is to blame for butter now costing four times as much. I came to know the price of everything—because I could never pay it—when I moved to the city, alone, as an apprentice of sixteen: hunger taught me the prices. The thought of fresh bread put me in a daze, and I would often roam the streets for hours in the evening thinking of nothing but—bread. My eyes smarted, my knees were weak, and I felt something wolflike inside me. Bread. I was addicted to bread as a person might be addicted to morphine. I was scared of myself, and I kept thinking of the man who had once come to the hostel and given a lecture with slides about a North Pole expedition and told us they had ripped apart the live fish they had just caught and devoured them raw. To this day, when I have picked up my pay and walk through town with the bills and coins in my pocket, I am often seized by the memory of the wolfish fear of those days, and I buy bread, fresh and warm as it lies in bakery windows: I buy two loaves that I find particularly attractive, then at the next bakery another, and little brown crisp rolls, far too many, which I later leave in the kitchen for my landlady because I can't eat a quarter of the bread I have bought and can't stand the idea that the bread might go bad.

The worst time for me had been the months just after Mother's death: I didn't feel like continuing my

20

electrician's apprenticeship, but I had already tried so many things: I had been a bank clerk, a sales clerk, and a carpenter's apprentice, each for exactly two months, and I hated this new job too, hated my employer so much that I often felt giddy when I rode back to the hostel in the evening on the overcrowded tram. But I stuck out the apprenticeship because I had made up my mind to show them.

Three or four evenings a week I was allowed to go to St Vincent's Hospital, where a distant relative of my mother's was the sister in charge of the kitchen. There I was given soup, and sometimes bread, and on the bench in front of the kitchen serving hatch I always found four or five other hungry fellows, mostly old men who stretched out their trembling hands when the shutter slid open and Sister Clara's round arms came into view, and I had to contol myself not to snatch the bowl of soup from her hand. This doling out of soup always took place late in the evening, long after the patients had gone to sleep— so they would not suspect that their rations were being used for unwarranted charity—and in the cor- ridor where we sat there were only two fifteen-watt bulbs to light up our meal. Quite often our sipping was interrupted, the shutter pushed back a second time, and Sister Clara would push plates of pudding through the opening: the pudding was always red, red like the candy sticks you get at the fair, and when we rushed to the serving hatch, Sister Clara would be standing on the far side of the kitchen, shaking her head, sighing, usually close to tears. Then she would say: "Wait," and go back again into the kitchen and return with a jug of custard sauce: the custard was a sulphurous yellow, yellow like the sun in a Sunday painter's picture. And we drank the soup, ate the pudding, ate the custard—and would wait to see whether the shutter would slide back again: sometimes there was a piece of bread as well, and once a month Sister Clara distributed her cigarette ration among us: each of us got one or two of those precious white objects—but usually Sister Clara only slid back the shutter to tell us there was nothing left. Every month the groups fed by Sister Clara were switched around, and we then got into another group that was allowed to come four times a week, and this fourth day was a Sunday: and on Sundays there were sometimes potatoes and gravy, and I yearned for the end of the month, to get into this other group, yearned like a prisoner waiting for the end of his sentence.

Ever since then I have hated the word "reasonable" because I always heard my employer use it: Wickweber was, I suppose, what is known as an upright man; he was competent, good at his trade, even good-natured in his own way. I was not quite sixteen when I entered his apprenticeship. At that time he had two helpers and four apprentices, as well as a master electrician who was usually at the small factory that Wickweber was just then starting up. Wickweber was a fine figure of a man, ruddy and robust, and even his piousness had its attractive side. At first I merely disliked him outright, but two months later the smells coming from his kitchen were enough to make me hate him: smells of things I had never tasted in my life, smells of freshly baked cake, of roasts and hot fat, and this beast grinding away in

my intestines, my hunger, found these smells un-
bearable, it reared up, and a sour hot taste would rise
in my throat, and I began to hate Wickweber because I went to work in the morning with two slices
of bread stuck together with red jam, and a pot of
cold soup that I was supposed to warm up at some
construction site but which I usually gulped down on
my way to work. Then when I turned up at work the
empty pot would rattle around in my toolbox, and I
counted on some woman customer giving me a piece
of bread, a plate of soup, or anything else edible. I
usually got something. In those days I was shy, taci-
turn, a tall, skinny boy, and nobody seemed to
know, or to notice, anything about the wolf living
inside me. Once I overheard a woman discussing me
without knowing I was listening; she spoke highly of
me and ended by saying: "He looks so distinguished." Fine, I thought at the time, so I look
distinguished, and I started examining myself more
closely in the mirror of the hostel washroom: I examined my pale, narrow face, thrust my lips forward, drew them back again, and thought: So that's
what a person looks like when he looks distinguished. And aloud I said to my own face there in
the mirror: "I need something to fill my belly. . . ."

In those days Father kept writing that he intended
coming to see how I lived, but he never did. When I
was at home he would ask me what things were like
in the city, and I had to tell him about the black
market, about the hostel, about my work, and he
would shake his head in dismay, and when I mentioned my hunger—I didn't do that often but sometimes it slipped out—Father would hurry off to the

kitchen and bring out everything edible he could find: apples, bread, margarine, and sometimes he would stand at the stove and slice cold potatoes into the pan and fry them up for me; once he came back helplessly holding a red cabbage and saying: "That's all I could find—I believe it can be made into a salad," but on those occasions I never enjoyed what I ate. I had a feeling of having committed an injustice or expressed myself badly, of having described conditions in the city in a way that did not correspond to the truth. I also used to quote him the price of bread, butter, and coal—and although each time it was a shock to him, he always seemed to forget it again; however, sometimes he sent me money to buy bread, and when Father's money arrived I would go to the black market, buy myself a whole two- or three-pound loaf, fresh from the bakery, sit down with it on a bench or somewhere among the ruins, break open the loaf in the middle, and eat it with my dirty hands, tearing off pieces and stuffing them into my mouth; sometimes it was still steaming, all warm inside, and for a few moments I had the sensation of holding a living creature in my hands, of tearing it to pieces, and I would think of the man who had given us the lecture on the North Pole expedition and told us they had torn apart live fish and devoured them raw. Often I would wrap up part of the bread in newspaper and put it in my tool bag, but then after walking on a hundred yards I would stop, unwrap it again, and swallow the rest, right there on the street. If it had been a three-pound loaf I would feel so full that at the hostel I would relinquish my supper to someone else and go straight to bed; and I would lie,

24

wrapped in my blankets, alone up there in the dormitory, my stomach full of sweet, fresh bread, satiated to the point of numbness. It would be eight in the evening, and I had eleven hours of sleep ahead of me, for I could never get enough sleep either.

Perhaps in those days Father felt indifferent to everything but Mother's illness; at any rate, I would try, when I was at home, to avoid the word hunger or any allusion to my plight, for I knew, and what's more I could see, that Father had much less to eat than I had; he was yellow in the face, thin and absentminded. Then we would go to visit Mother: she too always offered me something to eat when I sat by her bed, things she had saved from her meals or that she had been given by visitors: some fruit, or a bottle of milk, a piece of cake, but I couldn't eat anything because I knew she had T.B. and had to eat properly. But she would urge me and say it would go bad if I didn't eat it, and Father would say: "Clare, you must eat—you must get well again." Mother would cry, turn her head to one side, and I couldn't eat any of the things she offered me. In the next bed lay a woman in whose eyes I could see the wolf, and I knew that this woman would eat everything Mother left, and I could feel Mother's hot hands on my arm and see in her eyes the fear of her neighbour's greed. Mother would beseech me, saying: "My boy, please eat, I know you're hungry, and I know what it's like in the city." But I would just shake my head, squeeze her hand in return, and silently beseech her to stop urging me, and she would smile, say no more about food, and I knew she had understood. I said: "Maybe you'd do better at home, maybe you'd do

25

better in another room," but Mother said: "There are no other rooms, and they won't let me go home because I'm infectious." And later, when we spoke to the doctor, Father and I, I hated the doctor for his indifference: he was thinking of other things while he was talking to us, looking toward the door or out of the window while answering Father's questions, and I could tell from his red, finely curved lips that Mother was going to die.

But the woman lying next to Mother died first. When we arrived one Sunday at midday she had just died, the bed was empty, and her husband, who had evidently just been told, came into the ward and gathered up her belongings from the bedside table: hairpins and a powder compact, underwear and a box of matches; he did this in silence and in haste, without acknowledging our presence. He was a scrawny little man, with a face like a pike, a dark complexion, and button eyes, and when the ward sister came along he started shouting about a tin of meat he hadn't been able to find in the drawer of the bedside table. "Where's that corned beef?" he yelled at her. "I brought it for her last night when I came from work, at ten o'clock, and if she died during the night she couldn't have had time to eat it!" He brandished his wife's hairpins under the ward sister's nose, yellow foam flecked the corners of his mouth. He kept shouting: "Where's that meat? I want that meat! If I don't get that meat back, I'll tear the place apart!" The ward sister flushed deeply, started shouting too, and I thought from her expression that she had stolen the meat. The fellow was raving, he threw his wife's things on the floor and stamped on them, shouting: "I want that meat—you bunch of whores, thieves, murderers!" It lasted only a few seconds, then Father dashed out into the corridor to get help, and I planted myself between the man and the ward sister as he was starting to hit out at her; but he was short and quick on his feet, much quicker than I was, and he managed to strike the sister in the chest with his swarthy little fists. I could see him grinning through his rage, with bared teeth, the way I'd seen rats that had been caught in a trap in the hostel kitchen. "The meat, you whore!" he screamed, "the meat!" until Father turned up with two orderlies, who grabbed hold of him and dragged him out into the corridor, but even through the closed door we could still hear him screaming: "I want that meat back, you thieves!"

When silence had returned outside, we looked at each other, and Mother said quietly: "Every time he came they quarrelled about the money she gave him to buy food. He always shouted at her, saying prices had gone up again, and she never believed him. It was sickening, the things they used to say to each other, but she always gave him the money." Mother was silent, looking across to the bed of the woman who had died, then said softly: "They were married for twenty years, and their only son was killed in the war. Sometimes she took his photo from under her pillow and cried. It's still there, and her money too. He didn't find it. And the corned beef," she said, more softly still, "she did have time to eat it." And I tried to picture how it must have been: the dark, greedy woman, close to death, lying next to Mother in the night and eating the corned beef out of the tin.

27

Father wrote to me often in the years after Mother's death, more and more often, and his letters grew longer and longer. Usually he wrote that he would be coming to see how I lived, but he never did, and for seven years I lived alone in the city. When Mother died, he suggested I change my apprenticeship and look for one in Knochta, but I wanted to stay in town because I was beginning to find my feet, because I was beginning to get wise to Wickweber's dodges, and I was anxious to complete my apprenticeship with him. Besides, I had met a girl called Veronika; she worked in Wickweber's office, she was blonde and had a great big smile, I spent a lot of time with her. On summer evenings we used to stroll along the bank of the Rhine, or eat ice cream, and I would kiss her as we sat in the dark, down there on the blue basalt stones of the embankment, our bare feet dangling in the water. On clear nights we could see across the whole river, we would swim out to the wreck that lay in midchannel and sit on the iron bench where once the bargeman had sat in the evening with his wife. The living quarters that had been behind the bench had long since been dismantled, we could only lean against an iron bar. Down in the barge, the water gurgled. I met Veronika less often after she had been made redundant and Wickweber's daughter had taken over her job at the office. A year later she married a widower, the owner of a dairy shop, not far from the street where I now live. When my car is being serviced and I take the

28

tram, I can see Veronika at the back of the shop: she is still blonde, she still has a great big smile, but in her face I see the seven years that have passed. She has grown fat, and children's clothes hang on the washing line in the backyard: pink, that must be for a little girl, and blue, that must be for the boy. One day the door was open, and I could see her at the back of the shop ladling milk with her broad, handsome hands. She had sometimes brought me bread from a cousin who worked at a bakery; Veronika had insisted on feeding me, and each time she gave me a piece of bread I had those hands near my eyes. Once, however, I had shown her Mother's ring, and in her eyes I had caught the same greedy glint that had been in the eyes of the woman in the next bed to Mother's at the hospital.

During those seven years I became far too much aware of prices not to dislike the word "reasonable"; nothing is reasonable, and the price of bread is always a shade too high.

I had found my feet—if that's what it's called—I had mastered my trade to the point where I was no longer the low-priced labour I had been for Wickweber those last three years. I have a small car, all paid up, and for years I have been saving for that bond I want to keep up my sleeve so as to be independent of Wickweber and free to switch to the competition at any time. Most of the people I deal with are nice to me, as I am to them. It is all tolerable enough. I have my own price, the price of my hands, of my technical know-how, of a certain degree of experience, of my courteous relations with customers (known as I am for my charm and my impeccable manners, which come in especially handy because I am also an agent for those same washing machines that I have learned to repair in the dark), and I have been steadily able to increase this price—things couldn't be better for me—and meanwhile the price of bread has, one might say, been adjusted. I worked twelve hours a day, slept eight, and that left me four for what people call leisure: I would go out with Ulla, my boss's daughter; we weren't engaged, at least not "officially", but there was a tacit understanding that I would marry her. . . .

However, it was Sister Clara of St Vincent's Hospital, who gave me soup, bread, bright-red pudding, and sulphur-yellow custard, who gave me a total of maybe twenty cigarettes—the kind of pudding I would never eat today, the kind of cigarettes I would never smoke today—Sister Clara, who has been lying out there at the nuns' cemetery all these years: I feel more tenderness for the memory of her puffy face, her sad, watery eyes when she finally closed the serving hatch, than I feel for all the people I used to run into when I went out with Ulla. I could read in their eyes, see written in their hands, the prices I would have had to pay; I imagined myself without my own charm, took away their finery, their perfumes, all that "reasonably priced" *grandezza*, and I woke up the wolf that still slept inside me, the hunger that taught me the prices: I heard him growl when I danced cheek to cheek with a pretty girl, and I saw the dainty little hands resting on my arm or shoulder turn into claws that would have snatched away my bread. Not many people ever gave me anything: Father, Mother, and now and then the girls at the factory.

PART TWO

I DRIED my razor blade on one of those squares of paper, a pad of which is always hanging by a corner from a hook next to my washbasin; the salesman from the soap company gives them to me. The outside of the pad is printed with a woman's scarlet lips, and under the scarlet lips are the words: "Please do not wipe your lipstick on the towel." There are other pads of similar squares of paper, and the outside of these shows a man's hand cutting a towel with a razor blade; these are printed with the words "Use this paper for your razor blade" —but I prefer to use the ones with the scarlet lips, and the others I give away to my landlady's kids.

I picked up the roll of insulated wire that Wolf had brought over the previous evening, picked up the money from the desk where I empty my pockets every night, and as I was leaving my room the phone rang. My landlady said again: "Yes, I'll give him the message"—then she saw me and silently held out the receiver. I shook my head, but she nodded so emphatically that I went over and took the receiver. A tearful woman's voice said something, of which I understood only "Kurbel Street—please come, please please come!" I said: "Yes, I'll be along"— and the weeping woman again said something of which I only caught "quarrel . . . my husband . . . please come right away," and again I said: "Yes, I'll be along," and hung up.

"Don't forget the flowers," my landlady said, "and remember lunch. It'll be just about noon."

I forgot the flowers; I drove back into town from an outlying suburb, though I could have done another repair job in the neighbourhood and so charged mileage and driving time twice over. I drove fast because it was already half-past eleven and the train was due in at eleven forty-seven. I knew that train: I had often taken it back to town on Mondays after visiting Father. And on the way to the station I tried to picture the girl.

Seven years ago, when I was spending my last year at home, I had seen her a few times. During that year I had been in Muller's house exactly twelve times: once a month to deliver the modern-language journals that it had been my father's turn to read. Neatly entered at the bottom of the last page were the initials of the three modern-language teachers: Mu, that was Muller; Zbk, that was Zubanek; and Fen, that was for my father, from whom I have inherited the name Fendrich.

My most vivid recollection was of the dark patches on the walls of Muller's house: on the green stucco were black clouds caused by rising dampness, right up to the ground-floor windows, fantastic shapes that always looked to me like maps from some mysterious atlas. Towards summer they dried out at the edges and were fringed by wreaths of leprous white, but even during the heat of summer these clouds retained a dark-grey core. In winter and autumn the moisture would spread beyond these leprous borders, just like an ink blot spreading over blotting paper: black and acid. And I clearly recalled Muller's slippered informality, his rather sloppy habits, his long pipe, the leather spines of his books, and the photo in the hallway of Muller as a young man wearing a beribboned student's cap, and under this photo the insignia of the Teutonia or some other Onia fraternity. Occasionally I had run into Muller's son, who was two years younger than I; at some time or other he had been in my class but by now had advanced far beyond me. He was big-boned, his hair cut very short, and he looked like a bull calf. He always avoided spending more than a minute with me, for he was a decent fellow; he probably found my presence painful because of the effort to keep everything out of his voice that he felt might hurt me: pity, arrogance, and that embarrassing, artificial joviality. So, when we did meet, he confined himself to a hoarsely cheerful Hello and showed me directly to his father's room. Only twice had I seen a little girl of twelve or thirteen: the first time she was playing with some empty flowerpots in the garden; she had built a pyramid of the dry, light-red pots against the moss-green wall, and she gave a start when a woman's voice called "Hedwig!" and it looked as if her alarm imparted itself to the pile of flowerpots, for the topmost pot of her pyramid rolled down and shattered on the wet, dark cement paving of the courtyard.

On the other occasion she had been in the corridor that led to Muller's room: she had made a bed for her doll in a laundry basket, fair hair fell over her thin childish neck, which there in the corridor had almost a greenish tinge, and I could hear her humming a tune to the invisible doll, an unfamiliar tune to which at intervals she matched a single word: "Suvaya-su-su-Suvaya," and when I passed her on my way to Muller's room she looked up and I caught a glimpse of her face: she was pale and thin, and the fair hair hung in strands over her face. That must have been the girl Hedwig, for whom I had now found a room.

There are probably twenty thousand people in this city looking for the kind of room I was supposed to find for Muller's daughter, but only two such rooms exist, maybe even only one, and it is being rented out by one of those unrecognized angels who now and again go astray among human beings. I have such a room, I found it when I asked Father to take me out of the hostel. My room is large, furnished with a few old but comfortable pieces, and the four years I have been living there seem to me like an eternity: I have been in on the births of my landlady's children and am godfather to the youngest because I was the one who went out at night to fetch the midwife. For weeks on end, during the time when I was getting up early, I used to warm the milk for Robert and give him his bottle because my landlady, worn out by night work, slept late in the mornings and I hadn't the heart to wake her. Her husband is one of those whom the world is pleased to regard as an artist, a victim of circumstances: he complains for hours on end about his lost youth, stolen from him, he claims, by the war. "We were cheated," he says, "cheated of the best years in a man's life, the years from twenty to twenty-eight," and this lost youth provides him with an alibi for all kinds of nonsense that his wife not only forgives but even makes possible: he paints, designs buildings, composes. . . .

None of this—so it seems to me at least—does he do properly, although he occasionally makes some money at it. His designs hang in the rooms of the apartment: "House for an Author in the Taunus Hills", "House for a Sculptor", and all these designs are crowded with trees, the kind architects draw, and I detest architects' trees because I have been looking at them every day for four years. I swallow his advice the way one swallows medicine prescribed by a doctor who happens also to be a friend. "In this city," he may say, "in this city, living here alone as you do and at your age, I have had to face dangers I wouldn't wish on you," and then I know he is referring to the red-light district.

My landlady's husband is agreeable enough but— to my mind—a fool whose sole talent lies in retaining his wife's love and fathering delightful children. My landlady is tall and fair, and for a while I was so violently in love with her that I used secretly to kiss her apron, her gloves, and I couldn't sleep for jealousy of that fool of a husband of hers. But she loves him, and apparently a man needn't be smart or successful to be loved by such a woman—whom I still admire.

39

From time to time he touches me for a few marks so that he can go to one of those artists' cafés where he shows off with flapping tie and unkempt hair, finishing off a whole bottle of schnapps. I let him have the money because I am incapable of hurting his wife's feelings by humiliating him. And he knows why I do it, possessed as he is of that cunning without which loafers would starve. He is one of those loafers who know how to assume the air of great improvisers, but actually I doubt whether he knows how to improvise at all.

I always imagined I had got hold of one of those unique rooms, so I was all the more surprised to find one almost equally good for Muller's daughter in the centre of town in a building where I service laundry machines. I check the rubber parts for durability, replace hoses before they wear out, tighten screws before they get too loose. I love the downtown area: the districts over the last fifty years have changed owners and inhabitants like a tailcoat that, first put on for a wedding, was later worn by an impoverished uncle earning a bit on the side as a musician; pawned and not redeemed by his heirs, it was finally auctioned off by the pawnbroker and acquired by a costume rental agency, and the agency lets it for a moderate fee to impoverished patricians finding themselves invited to a reception for some diplomat whose country they search for in vain in their youngest son's atlas.

There, in the building that houses a laundry, I had found a room for Muller's daughter that corresponded almost exactly to his specifications: it was quite large, not badly furnished, and it had a large window overlooking the garden of one of the old patrician villas; here, in the heart of town, after five in the afternoon it was peaceful and quiet.

I took the room from the first of February. Then I struck a snag because Muller wrote me at the end of January that his daughter was sick and couldn't come till March the fifteenth, and couldn't I arrange for the landlady to hold the room without charging rent. I wrote him a furious letter, telling him what the housing situation in town was like, and then I was ashamed at how humbly he replied and agreed to pay the rent for six weeks.

I had scarcely thought of the girl again, beyond making sure that Muller had actually paid the rent. He had sent it, and when I inquired about it the land-lady asked me the same question as before, when I went to look at the room. "Is she your girl friend? Are you sure she's not your girl friend?"

"For God's sake," I said in annoyance, "I've told you: I don't even know the girl."

"You see, I won't allow," she said, "any . . ."

"I know," I said, "what you won't allow, but I'm telling you, I don't know the girl."

"Very well," she said. I hated her for her smirk. "I'm only asking because I sometimes make an exception for engaged couples."

"For God's sake," I said, "now you've got us engaged! You really don't have to worry." But she still seemed to be worrying.

I was a few minutes late getting to the station, and while I dropped my coin into the machine for a plat-form ticket, I tried to recall the girl who so long ago had sung "Suvaya" as I carried the modern-language journals along the dark corridor to Muller's room. I stood by the stairs leading up to the platform and thought: Blonde, age twenty, coming to town to be a schoolteacher; as I eyed the people walking past, the world seemed full of blonde twenty-year-old girls—there were so many coming off this train, and they were all carrying suitcases and looked as if they were coming to town to become teachers. I was too tired to speak to any of them. I lit a cigarette and crossed over to the other side of the stairs, and there I saw a girl sitting behind the railing on a suitcase, a girl who must have been sitting behind me the whole time: she had dark hair, and her coat was as green as grass that has sprouted during a warm rainy night; it was so green I felt it must smell of grass. Her hair was dark, like slate roofs after rain, her face white, startlingly white, like fresh whitewash with a bit of ochre shimmering through it. I thought she was wearing makeup, but she wasn't. I saw only that bright-green coat, that face, and suddenly I was filled with fear, that fear explorers must feel when they step onto new land, knowing that another expedition is on the way, might have already planted its flag, taken possession; explorers who, after the ordeal of the long journey, all its hardships, the gamble of life and death, must fear that their struggle might have been in vain.

That face sank deeply into me, penetrating through and through like a die striking wax instead of silver bars, and it felt as if I were being pierced without bleeding; for one insane moment I felt an urge to destroy that face, the way an artist destroys the plate from which he has taken only a single print.

I dropped my cigarette and hurried over to her. My fear had left me when I stood facing her. I said: "D'you need any help?"

She smiled, nodded, and said: "Oh yes, you can tell me how to get to Juden Lane."

"Juden Lane," I said, and it was as if I were hearing my name being called in a dream without recognizing it as my name; I was outside my senses, and I seemed to understand what it means to be outside one's senses.

"Juden Lane," I said, "right, Juden Lane. Come along." I watched her stand up and lift the heavy suitcase in slight surprise, and I was too dazed to realize that I should have carried it; I was far beyond the usual courtesies. The realization, which at that moment had not yet quite sunk in—the realization that she was Hedwig Muller, which should have come to me automatically when she said "Juden Lane"—almost drove me out of my mind. Something had got mixed up or gone wrong: I was so sure that Muller's daughter was blonde, that she was one of the innumerable blonde teacher-candidates who had been walking past me, that I could not identify this girl with her, and to this day I often wonder whether she really is Hedwig Muller, and I hesitate to say that name because I feel I still have to discover hers. "That's right," I said in reply to her questioning look, "just come with me," and I let her walk ahead with the heavy suitcase and followed her to the barrier.

In that half-minute during which I walked behind her I was thinking that I would possess her and that, in order to possess her, I would destroy anything that might stand in my way. I saw myself wrecking washing machines, smashing them to pieces with a ten-pound hammer. I looked at Hedwig's back, her neck, her hands drained of blood from carrying the heavy suitcase. I was jealous of the ticket collector who briefly touched her hand as she held out her rail-pass—jealous of the station floor beneath her feet. I didn't think of taking the suitcase from her till we had almost reached the main exit. "I'm sorry," I said, stepping to her side and taking the suitcase from her.

"It's nice of you to come and pick me up."

"Good heavens," I said, "do you know who I am?"

"Of course I do," she said with a laugh, "your picture stands on your father's desk."

"You know my father?"

"Yes," she said, "he was one of my teachers."

I lifted her suitcase into the back seat of the car, put her handbag beside it, and helped her get in, and that's how I first came to hold her hand and her elbow: it was a round, firm elbow, and a broad hand, but light—dry and cool—and as I walked around to the other side of the car to get in behind the wheel I stopped by the radiator, opened the bonnet, and pretended to look inside: but I was looking at her as she sat behind the windscreen. I was afraid, but now it wasn't the fear that someone else might discover and conquer her; that fear was gone, for I wasn't going to move from her side, not this day nor on the many days that were to come, all the days that add up to a lifetime. It was a different fear, fear of what was to

44

come: the train I had intended to take stood ready to leave, its steam was up, the other passengers were already inside, the signal had been raised, and the man in the red cap had already lifted his green disc, and everyone was waiting for me, as I stood there on the step, to jump on board, but at that very moment I was already jumping off. I thought of all those frank discussions I would have to endure, and I knew that I had always detested frank discussions: endless, pointless talk and the pointless weighing of guilt and innocence, reproaches, nagging, phone calls, letters, guilt I was going to bear—guilt I already bore. I saw that other, that tolerable life running on like some complicated machine set up for someone who was no longer there: I was no longer there; screws came loose, pistons overheated, metal parts sailed through the air, and there was a smell of burning.

I had long since closed the bonnet again, my arms were braced against the metal grille, and I was looking through the windscreen at her face, which was divided into two unequal parts by one of the windscreen wipers. It seemed incredible that no man had yet noticed how beautiful she was, that no one had yet recognized her: but perhaps it was because she didn't exist till the moment I looked at her.

She glanced up at me as I got in and sat down beside her, and I could see in her eyes the fear of what I might say, what I might do, but I said nothing; without a word I started the car and drove into town; only at times, when I made a right turn, I could see her profile, and I eyed her from the side, and she was eyeing me too. I drove to Juden Lane and had already slowed the car to stop outside the building where she was to live, but I still didn't know what I was going to do when we stopped, got out, and went inside—so I drove right through Juden Lane, made a wide circle through town with her in the car, came back again to the station, and drove once more to Juden Lane, and this time I stopped.

I said nothing as I helped her out of the car and held her broad hand again and felt her round elbow cupped in my left hand. I took the suitcase, walked to the front door, rang the bell, and didn't look back at her as she followed with her handbag. I ran ahead with the suitcase, put it down upstairs by the apartment door, and met her as she was coming slowly up the stairs carrying her handbag. I didn't know how to address her—neither Hedwig nor Miss Muller seemed appropriate—so I said: "I'll be back in half an hour to take you to lunch, all right?"

She merely nodded, gazing thoughtfully past me, and she seemed to have something on her mind. I said no more, ran down the stairs, got into my car, and drove off with no idea of where I was going. I don't remember what streets I drove along or what I was thinking about, I only know the car seemed inexpressibly empty, the car I almost always drive in alone, except occasionally with Ulla, and I tried to remember what it had been like an hour earlier when I drove to the station without Hedwig.

But all that had gone before had been wiped from my memory: I saw myself alone in my car driving to the station, as you see an identical twin brother with whom you have nothing in common except the likeness. I didn't come to my senses till I found myself driving straight towards a florist's; I stopped the car and went in. It was cool inside, there was a sweet smell of blossoms, and I was alone. There should be green roses, I thought, roses with green petals, and I saw myself in the mirror, taking out my wallet, picking out the money—I didn't recognize myself in the mirror right away, and I flushed because I had thought "Green roses" out loud, and now I felt I had been overheard—I only recognized myself by the flush rising in my face, and I thought: So that's really you, you really do look quite distinguished. An elderly woman emerged from the back; I could see her false teeth smiling and shining way off: she was still swallowing a mouthful of her lunch, and after the swallow her smile was right there again, yet it had seemed as if she had been swallowing her smile too. I could tell from her face that she was classifying me as a red-rose customer, and with a smile she went over to a great bouquet of red roses standing in a silver bucket. Her fingers just barely caressed the blooms, there was something indecent about it, and I thought of the brothels that Mr Brotig, my landlady's husband, had warned me about, and I suddenly knew why I felt so uncomfortable: it was like being in a brothel.

"Lovely, aren't they?" said the woman. But I didn't want the red roses, I had never liked them. "White ones," I said hoarsely—and with a smile she went over to another bucket, a bronze one, containing white roses. "Ah," she said, "for a wedding."

"That's right," I said, "for a wedding."

I had two notes and some loose change in my jacket pocket; I put it all on the counter and said (just as, when I was a kid, I had put my pfennigs on the counter and said: "Sweets, please, for all this"): "White roses, please, for all this—and plenty of green." The woman took the money with the tips of her fingers, counted it out onto the counter, and calculated on some wrapping paper how many roses I was entitled to. She did not smile while she was calculating, but as she walked over to the bronze bucket that held the white roses her smile was suddenly there again, the way a hiccup is suddenly there again. The pungent sweetness filling the air in the florist's suddenly went to my head like a deadly poison, and I made two long strides to the counter, scooped up my money, and ran out.

I jumped into my car—simultaneously seeing myself from an infinite distance jumping into the car like someone who has just robbed a till—drove off, and when I saw the station ahead I felt I had seen it a thousand times a day for a thousand years, yet the station clock showed ten minutes past twelve, and it had been a quarter to twelve when I dropped my coin into the machine for the platform ticket: I seemed still to hear the growl of the machine swallowing it, and the light, sneering click with which it spat out the cardboard ticket, and in the meantime I had forgotten who I was, what I looked like, and what I did for a living.

I drove around the station, stopped at the flower stall outside the Trade Bank, got out, and bought three marks' worth of yellow tulips: there were ten, and I gave the woman another three marks and bought ten more. I took the flowers to the car, threw them onto the back seat beside my toolbox, walked past the flower stall into the Trade Bank, and when I

48

drew my chequebook from the inside pocket of my jacket and slowly walked to the desk facing the cashier, I felt somewhat ridiculous; besides, I was afraid they wouldn't pay out my money. On the green cover of the chequebook I had made a note of my balance: 1,710.80, and I slowly wrote out the cheque, writing 1,700 in the little space at the top right, and seventeen hundred on the line after "in words". And when I signed my name at the bottom of the cheque, Walter Fendrich, I felt like a person committing a forgery. I was still scared as I handed the cheque to the girl beside the cashier, but she took it without looking at me, threw it on a moving belt, and handed me a yellow numbered disc. I waited beside the cashier, watched the cheques returning to the cashier on another moving belt, and mine came quickly too: I was surprised when the cashier called my number, I pushed the disc towards him across the white marble surface, and the money was paid out to me—ten hundreds and fourteen fifties.

I felt strange as I left the bank with the money in my pocket: it was my money, I had saved it, and it hadn't been hard to save it since I had been doing well, but the white marble pillars, the gilded door I went out through onto the street, the stern, solemn look on the face of the doorman—all these made me feel as if I had stolen my own money.

But when I got into the car I laughed and drove quickly back to Juden Lane.

I rang Mrs Grohlta's bell, pushed the door open with my back when the buzzer sounded, and walked up the stairs, weary and despairing; I was afraid of what was to come. I carried the flowers upside down, like a sack of potatoes. I walked straight ahead, without looking right or left. I don't know what kind of face the landlady made as I passed her—I didn't look at her.

Hedwig was sitting by the window holding a book, I saw at once that she had not been reading it: I had crept quietly along the corridor to her door and opened it—as silently as thieves open doors (yet I had never practised this, never learned it from anyone). She snapped the book shut, and I can no more forget that little gesture than I can forget her smile; I can still hear the two halves of the book slapping together—this made the railway ticket, which she was using as a bookmark, flutter out, and neither she nor I, neither one of us bent down to pick it up.

I did not move from the door, I looked at the old trees in the garden, at Hedwig's clothes, which she had unpacked and strewn over table and chair, and on the book were the words, clearly visible in red on green, *Basics of Teaching*. She was standing between bed and window, her arms hanging down, hands slightly clenched, like someone about to beat a drum who has not yet gripped the drumsticks. I was looking at her, but I was not thinking about her at all; I was thinking about what Wickweber's assistant, the one I had always worked with as a first-year apprentice, had told me. He was called Grömmig, he was tall and thin, and his forearm was covered with scars from hand-grenade splinters. During the war he had sometimes put a towel over the faces of women he was possessing, and I had been surprised by how little his descriptions revolted me. My revulsion at

50

Grömmig's description came only now, as I stood there facing Hedwig, holding the flowers: six years later and what Grömmig had told me seemed worse than anything I had ever had to listen to. The assistants had told me many disgusting things, but not one of them had covered a woman's face with a towel— and those who hadn't now seemed to me as innocent as children. Hedwig's face—I could hardly think of anything else.

"Go away," she said, "go at once."

"Yes," I said, "I'm going," but I didn't move; the thing I wanted to do with her now was something I had never done with any woman; there were many words for it, many expressions, and I knew almost all of them, I had learned them during my apprentice years, at the hostel, and from the other students at the engineering school, but not one of those expressions fitted what I wanted to do with her now— and I am still searching for the word. "Love" is not the word that expresses all of it, perhaps it is only the one that comes closest.

I could read in Hedwig's face what could be read in mine: alarm and fear, nothing of what is known as desire, yet everything that men who had talked to me about it had never found—and suddenly I knew that this even included Grömmig: behind the towel that he had used to cover the woman's face he had been looking for beauty, all he had to do—it seemed to me—was take away the towel and he would have found it. Slowly that which had fallen from my face over Hedwig's face dropped away, and I saw her face emerge again, the face that had so deeply penetrated my being.

"You must go," she said.

"D'you like the flowers?" I asked.

"Yes."

I laid them on her bed, still wrapped in paper, and watched as she unwrapped them, arranged the buds, plucked at the green. One would think she were given flowers every day.

"Pass me that vase, will you?" she said, and I passed her the vase that was on the chest of drawers beside me near the door: she took a few steps towards me, and as she took the vase from me our hands touched for an instant, and during that instant I thought of all the things I might have tried: pull her towards me, kiss her and not let her go, but I didn't try, I stood with my back to the door again and watched her pour water from a jug into the vase and put the flowers in it: it was a dark-red ceramic vase, and the flowers looked very nice as she placed them in the window.

"You'd better go," she said again, and I turned without a word, opened the door, and went out along the corridor. It was dark here because the corridor had no window, there was only the dim grey light from the frosted-glass panel of the apartment door. I was hoping she would follow me and call out something, but she didn't, and I opened the apartment door and walked down the stairs.

At the building entrance I stopped, smoked a cigarette, looked out onto the sunny street, and read the name plates: "Hühnert", "Schmitz", "Stephanides", "Kroll"—then came her landlady's name: "Grohlta", and a printed card: "Flink Launderette"—that was the laundry.

Before finishing my cigarette I crossed the street

and stopped on the other side, looked back, and kept my eye on the doorway. I gave a start when suddenly the owner of the laundry, Mrs Flink, spoke to me: she must have crossed the street in her white overall, but I hadn't seen her.

"Oh, Mr Fendrich," she said, "you couldn't have come at a better time: one of the machines is over-heating, the girl has done something wrong."

"Switch if off," I said without looking at her. I kept on staring at the doorway.

"Couldn't you take a look at least?"

"No," I said, "I can't take a look."

"But you're standing right here!"

"Yes, I'm standing right here," I said, "but I can't take a look at the machine: I have to stand here."

"Well, if that isn't the limit!" said Mrs Flink. "You're standing right here, and you can't even take a quick look at the machine."

Out of the corner of my eye I saw Mrs Flink go back across the street, and a minute later the girls working for her appeared in the entrance to the laundry, four or five white overalls. I could hear the girls laughing, I didn't care.

This is what it must be like, I thought, to be drowning: grey water runs into you, a lot of water; you see nothing more, hear nothing more, only a muffled roar, and the grey, stale-tasting water seems sweet to you.

My brain went on working, like a machine some-one has forgotten to switch off: suddenly I found the solution to an algebra problem I hadn't been able to solve two years earlier during an exam at engineering school, and finding the solution filled me with the deep happiness you feel at suddenly recalling a name or a word you have been searching for a long time.

French words I hadn't known at school nine years ago came to my mind, and all at once I knew that "match" was *allumette*. "Pierre brought his father a match, and Pierre's father lit his pipe with the match. The fire was burning in the fireplace, and Pierre's father put new logs on before starting to tell him about his days in Indochina." A log is called *bûche,* and now I could have translated the sentence that at the time was beyond all of us, even our top student. It was as though someone in a dream were whispering words in my ear, words I had never read and never heard. But my eyes were riveted on one single image: the doorway of the building from which, at some time or other, Hedwig must emerge: it was a new door, painted brown, and I felt as if I had never seen anything but that door.

I don't know whether I was suffering: the waters closed over me, dark grey, and at the same time I was more wide awake than I had ever been: it occurred to me that some time or other I would have to apologize to Mrs Flink; she had always been nice to me, had got me the room for Hedwig, and sometimes, when I was tired, made me a cup of coffee. Some time or other, I thought, you'll have to apologize to her. There were a lot of things I had to do, and I thought of them all, even the woman on Kurbel Street who had wept into the phone and was still waiting for me.

I knew now what I had always known but hadn't admitted to myself for the last six years: that I hated this job, as I hated every job I had tried my hand at. I hated these washing machines, and I was filled with a disgust for the smell of soapy water, a disgust that was more than physical. All I liked about this job was the money it brought me, and that money I had in my pocket; I felt for it, it was still there.

I smoked another cigarette, and even that I did mechanically: taking the packet from my pocket, tapping out the cigarette, and then for a moment I saw the door shining red through the little flame of my lighter, saw it wreathed in the bluish smoke of my cigarette, but the cigarette didn't taste right, and I threw it, half smoked, into the gutter. Then, when I wanted to light up another, I could tell from the weight of the packet that it was empty, and I dropped it into the gutter too.

The fact also that I was hungry, that a slight nausea was circulating within me like liquid in a distilling flask—all that seemed to be happening outside me. I had never been able to sing, but here, across from the doorway from which, at some time or other, Hedwig must emerge—here I could have sung: I knew it.

I had always known that Wickweber, while keeping within the law, was a crook, but only now, standing on the roughened basalt curb across from that doorway, did I realize what the formula for the fraud had been: for two years I had worked in his factory; later it had been my job to inspect and approve the appliances manufactured there, appliances whose selling price I had myself worked out, together with Wickweber and Ulla. The material was cheap, and it was good, as good as the material used for submarines and aircraft, and Wickweber got it by the carload, and we worked out the retail price of a hot-water boiler at ninety marks. That was the price of three loaves of bread when the market was—as they used to say—somewhat saturated; and it was the price of two loaves when the market was—as they used to say—spongy. And I had personally tested the boilers in the cubbyhole above the payroll office and had stamped them with my F and the date before the apprentice took them to the warehouse to be packed in oil paper—and a year ago I had bought a boiler for my father which Wickweber let me have at the factory price, and the warehouse foreman had taken me into the warehouse, where I picked one out. I loaded it into my car, took it to Father, and when I installed it I discovered my stamped F and the date: 19/2/47—and it had felt strange, and I had turned it over in my mind like a formula that lacks some unknown quantity, and now, here on the curb across from Hedwig's doorway, it no longer seemed strange, and I had found the unknown quantity: what in those days had cost three loaves of bread was now being sold for the price of two hundred loaves, and even I, who got a discount, was still paying enough to buy a hundred and thirty loaves—and I was surprised that it was so much: that the unknown quantity represented so great a value, and I thought of all the electric irons, boilers, water heaters, and ranges that over the past two years I had stamped with my F.

I thought of my resentment, years ago, when I had gone to the Alps one winter with my parents. Father had taken a photo of Mother against a background of snow-covered peaks, she had dark hair and was wearing a light-coloured coat. I had stood beside her when he took the picture: everything had been white, only Mother's hair was dark—but when Father showed me the negative at home it looked as though a white-haired Negro woman was standing in front of great mounds of coal. I was indignant, and the chemical explanation, which was not even very complicated, didn't satisfy me. It had always seemed to me—and still did—that it couldn't be explained by a few chemical formulas, by solutions and salts, whereas I was intoxicated by the word "darkroom"—and later, to appease me, Father photographed my mother in a black coat standing in front of the coal mounds just outside town—there on the negative I saw a white-haired Negro woman in a white coat standing in front of immense mountains of snow; the only thing that was dark was the only light part of Mother: her white face, whereas her black coat and the coal mounds all looked as light, as festive, as if my mother were standing smiling in an expanse of snow.

My resentment was just as great after this second snapshot, and ever since then, photographic prints have not interested me, I have always felt that prints should never be made of photos, they were the very things that were the least truthful: it was the negatives I wanted to see, and I was fascinated by the darkroom where under a reddish light Father floated the negatives in mysterious trays until the snow turned into snow and coal into coal—but it was bad snow and bad coal—and it seemed to me that the snow on the negatives had been good coal and the coal on the negatives good snow. Father had tried to console me by saying that there was only one true print of everything, and that lay in a darkroom that we did not know: in God's memory—and at the time this explanation seemed too simple, because God was such a big word, one that grown-ups used to try and cover up everything.

But here, standing on the curb, I felt that I understood Father: I knew I was being photographed, just as I stood there: that there was a picture of me, as I stood there—so far below the surface of the grey water—there was a picture of me, and I longed to see that picture. If someone had spoken to me in French, I could have answered him in French, and here on the curb, across from Hedwig's building, I realized something that I had always been too scared to analyse, too shy to tell anyone: that it deeply mattered to me to arrive at evening mass before the Oblation, and just as deeply to remain in my seat afterwards while the church was emptying, often long enough for the verger to rattle his keys ostentatiously just as waiters will ostentatiously pile chairs on tables when they want to close up, and the sadness of having to leave the restaurant is not unlike the sadness I had felt at being kicked out of the church that I had entered at the very last minute. I felt that now I understood what it had so far been impossible for me to understand: that Wickweber could be devout and still a crook and that both were genuine: devout and crooked, and I let go of my hatred for him, like a child with a balloon who has been desperately clutching it all one summer Sunday afternoon—then suddenly lets go, to watch it rise into the evening sky where it gets smaller, smaller, until it is out of sight. I heard my own gentle sigh as I suddenly breathed out my hatred for Wickweber.

Good riddance, I thought, and for a moment I took my eyes off the door and tried to follow my sigh—and for that moment the place where my hatred had been turned into an empty space, a very slight nothingness that seemed to buoy me up as an air bladder buoys up a fish, just for that one moment, then I felt the space filling with something as heavy as lead: with an indifference of deadening weight. From time to time I also glanced at my watch, but I never looked at the hour or the minute hand, I looked only at the tiny circle that seemed to have been placed haphazardly above the six: there and there only did time move on for me, that quick, thin finger down there alone moved me on, not the big slow ones above, and that quick, thin finger moved rapidly, a small, precise machine, cutting slices out of something invisible, out of time, and it ground and drilled its way around in that nothingness, and the dust it drilled out of the nothingness fell over me like a magic substance that turned me into an immovable pillar.

I saw the girls from the laundry go off for lunch, saw them return. I saw Mrs Flink standing in the entrance to the laundry, saw her shake her head. People passed behind me, people passed the doorway from which Hedwig had to emerge, people who momentarily obscured the doorway, and I thought of all the things I should have been doing: the names of five customers were on the slip of white paper lying in my car, and at six I had a date with Ulla at Café Joos, but my thoughts kept bypassing Ulla.

59

It was Monday, March the fourteenth, and Hedwig did not appear. I held the watch to my left ear and could hear the mocking, industrious little second hand grinding holes into that nothingness, dark, circular holes that were beginning to dance before my eyes and gather around the doorway, to separate again and vanish in the blue sky like coins being thrown into the water; for a few moments my field of vision was pierced like one of those metal sheets from which I had punched out the square nickel blanks in Wickweber's factory, and in each of those holes I saw the doorway, saw it a hundred times, always the same doorway, tiny but precise doorways connected by thin perforations like a big sheet of stamps: the face of the inventor of the spark plug multiplied a hundred times over.

In my perplexity I searched my pockets for cigarettes, knowing I had none left, although there was another packet in the car, but the car was parked twenty yards to the right of the doorway and there was something like an ocean between me and the car. And I thought again of the woman on Kurbel Street who had wept into the phone as only women weep who can't cope with machines, and all at once I knew there was no further point in avoiding Ulla in my thoughts, so I thought about her: I did it the way you suddenly decide to turn the light on in a room where someone has died: in the half-light, it was possible to believe he was asleep, possible to persuade yourself that you could still hear him breathe, see him move; but now the light falls harshly on the scene, and you can see that preparations for the funeral have already been made: the candelabra are in place, the potted palms—and somewhere to the left below the dead person's feet there is a hump where the black cloth bulges incongruously: that's where the undertaker has placed the hammer in readiness to nail down the coffin lid tomorrow, and you can already hear what won't be heard till tomorrow: that final, naked hammering that has no tune.

The fact that Ulla didn't know yet made thinking about her all the worse: already there was nothing more to be changed, nothing more to be undone—anymore than you can pull the nails out of the coffin lid—but she didn't know yet.

I thought about the life I would have had with her; she had always looked at me the way you look at a hand grenade that has been converted into an ashtray and now stands on the piano: you tap the ash into it on Sundays after your cup of coffee, you clean it on Mondays, and as you clean it you keep experiencing that same little shiver: seeing what was originally such a dangerous object now performing such a harmless function, especially since the joker who made the ashtray has used the pin with such originality: you can pull the white china knob that looks like the knob of a bedside lamp—and that activates a hidden battery which causes a few little wires to glow, and from this glow you light your cigarette: a peaceful instrument now that had been manufactured for such unpeaceful purposes: you can pull the knob nine hundred and ninety-nine times without coming to any harm, but nobody knows that at the thousandth time a hidden mechanism is set off that makes the amusing toy explode. Nothing very terrible happens, a few scraps of metal fly around the room but won't actually penetrate the heart, you're startled, and from now on you treat it more cautiously.

Nor would anything very terrible happen to Ulla, and her heart wouldn't suffer, but everything except her heart would. She would talk, talk a lot, and I knew exactly what she would say; in a way that didn't matter she would be in the right and would want to be in the right, and she would gloat a little too, and I had always hated people who were right and gloated when they turned out actually to have been right: they always seemed to me like people who subscribe to a newspaper but always overlook something in the masthead about "Act of God"— and then show an unseemly indignation when one morning the newspaper fails to appear. As with insurance policies, they should have read the fine print more carefully than the headlines.

Only when I could no longer see the doorway did I remember what I was waiting for: for Hedwig. I could no longer see the door, it was hidden by a large, dark-red van that was very familiar to me: "Wickweber's Service Company" was painted on it in cream letters, and I went across the street because I had to see that doorway again. I walked slowly, like someone walking under water, and I sighed, as someone might sigh who, walking through forests of seaweed and colonies of shells, past astonished fish, has slowly climbed the steep bank as if it were a mountain and finds to his surprise that he no longer feels the weight of the column of water on the back of his neck but instead the lightness of the column of air that we take too much for granted.

I walked around the van, and when I could see the doorway again I knew Hedwig wasn't going to come down: she was lying up there on the bed, completely covered by the invisible dust that the second hand was grinding out of nothingness.

I was glad she had sent me away when I turned up with the flowers, and I was glad when she had known at once what I wanted to do with her, and I was scared of the moment when she would no longer send me away, a moment that would come sometime on a day that was still that Monday.

I no longer cared about the doorway, and I felt foolish, almost as foolish as I had been when I used to kiss my landlady's apron in secret. I walked to my car, opened the door, and took out the packet of cigarettes lying in the glove compartment under the receipt pad for mileage and work hours. I lit a cigarette, closed the car door, and couldn't decide what to do: whether to go up to Hedwig's room or drive out to the woman on Kurbel Street who had wept so copiously into the phone.

Suddenly Wolf's hand was on my shoulder: I felt it as I had felt the weight of the column of water, and by looking to the left I could even see the hand: it was the hand that had offered me countless cigarettes, accepted countless cigarettes from me, a clean and capable hand, and I could even see the engagement ring glinting in the March sunshine. From the slight trembling movement of the hand I could tell that Wolf was laughing—that soft, inward, chuckling laugh with which he used to laugh at our teacher's jokes at engineering school, and in the second before I turned toward him I could feel what I had once felt when Father persuaded me to take part in a reunion of my former classmates: I saw them all sitting there, the fellows with whom I had shared three, four, six, or nine years of my life, with whom I had crouched in the air-raid shelter while the bombs were falling; written tests had been the battles which, shoulder to shoulder, we had survived; together we had put out the fire in the burning school building and bandaged the injured Latin teacher, together we had carried him away, together we had flunked our year, and it seemed as though these experiences would form an eternal bond among us—but there was no bond, much less an eternal one, and the only memory left is the flat taste of that first cigarette smoked in secret, and the desire to put your hand on the arm of the waitress bringing your beer, a person seen for the very first time and who suddenly seems like an old acquaintance, almost as familiar as your mother— compared with the sense of alienation felt towards those others whose entire wisdom consists of having lost their ideals, ideals you have never had, ideals you begin to cherish because the others have lost them: wretched fools who all exaggerate a little when asked how much they earn a month—and suddenly you realize that the only friend you ever had was the one who died in Grade 11: Jürgen Brolaski, the boy you never exchanged a word with because he seemed so unattractive, so moody; drowned while swimming one summer evening, caught under a raft, down by the sawmill where the willows have split the blue basalt of the embankment, where a kid could roller skate in his swimming trunks down the concrete ramps used for hauling up lumber—on roller skates right down into the water; weeds between the paving stones and the ineffectual "That's enough—that's enough now!" of the night watchman who was gathering wood for his stove. Brolaski with his thin, angular body had no roller skates, his swimming trunks were pink, made by his mother out of an old petticoat, and sometimes I wondered whether he swam all the time just so we wouldn't see his trunks: only for brief moments would he climb up onto the raft, sit down, arms crossed over his thighs, his face to the Rhine, looking into the dark-green shadow of the bridge that in the evening stretched all the way to the sawmill; no one had seen him jump into the water, no one missed him till that evening his mother ran weeping through the streets, from house to house: "Have you seen my boy, have you seen Jürgen?" "No."

Brolaski's father stood beside the grave in his uniform, a private soldier with no decorations; he raised his head, listening pensively, when we started to sing: "Into an early grave, Brother, into an early grave hath Death now summoned thee, into an early grave. . . ."

All through the class reunion I could think only of Brolaski, and of the waitress's pretty white arm I longed to put my hand on; of Brolaski's pink swimming trunks, cut out of his mother's petticoat, held up by a wide piece of garter elastic: there in the dark-green shadow of the bridge Brolaski had vanished. . . .

"Brother, into an early grave hath Death now summoned thee, into an early grave. . . ."

Slowly I turned towards Wolf and looked into his

good, trustworthy face, which I had known for seven years, and I felt a bit ashamed, just as I had felt ashamed when Father had caught me stealing the blank report form.

"You've got to help me," said Wolf. "I can't figure out what's wrong. Do come." He took me by the hand, carefully, as one guides a blind man, and led me slowly to the laundry. I could smell what I smelled so often every day: the smell of dirty laundry, saw piles of it lying around—и д I saw the girls, saw Mrs Flink, all standing there in their overalls, just like after an explosion when through the cloud of dust you see all the people you had thought were dead.

"Overheated," he said, "tried three times—nothing—and all the machines—the whole lot."

"Did you remove the filters?" I asked Wolf.

"Yes, they were dirty, I cleaned them and put them back in—and all the machines overheated again."

"I'll lose my best customer," said Mrs Flink. "The Hotel Hunnenhof—the Hunnenhof's my best customer, and I'll lose them if the sheets aren't ready by this evening."

"Unscrew the hoses," I told Wolf, and I watched him unscrewing them from all four machines, at the same time I could hear the girls talking about the sheets, which they gossip about with the hotel chambermaids: many a time they had triumphantly shown me the smears of lipstick on the sheets used by politicians or actors, had held sheets out for me to sniff the perfume used by the mistress of some Party functionary—and all this had amused me, but

66

suddenly I knew how little I cared about politicians and Party functionaries: not even their private lives interested me, and the secrets of their private lives were welcome to run down the drain with the waste water coming out of the machines. I wanted to get out, I hated the machines, hated the smell of soapy water. . . .

Wolf had unscrewed all the hoses and looked at me helplessly, his expression a bit foolish.

"Have they been repairing the water main?" I asked Mrs Flink, without looking at her.

"Yes," she said, "yesterday they tore up Korbmacher Lane, that's where we get our water from."

"Yes," said Wolf, who had been letting the water run, "the water's all rusty and dirty."

"Let it run till it's clear, screw the hoses back on, and everything'll be okay. You won't lose your best customer," I told Mrs Flink, "the laundry'll be ready by this evening," and I left, went out again onto the street, as one passes in a dream from one landscape into another.

I sat down on the running board of Wickweber's van, but instead of staring at the doorway I closed my eyes and looked for an instant into the darkroom, seeing the image of the only person who I know has never shouted, never bawled out another person—the only person whose devoutness I have found convincing: I saw Father. In front of him was the little blue wooden box we used to keep our dominoes in. The box is always stuffed with memo slips, all cut by Father to the same size from waste paper; paper is the only thing he hoards. From letters begun and then discarded, from copybooks not fully used up, he cuts out the blank parts, from wedding and death announcements he cuts off the unprinted parts, and as for those impressive circulars, those requests on deckle-edged paper to appear at some rally or other, those invitations on linen paper to do something for the cause of Liberty—this printed matter fills him with childish delight because each one yields him at least six memo slips, which he then deposits as treasures in the old domino box. He is obsessed by bits of paper, inserts them in his books, his wallet bulges with them, matters both important and trivial are all confided to these slips. I was forever coming across them when I was still living at home. "Button on undershorts" was written on one of them, on another "Mozart", on another "pillageuse—pillage," and once I found one saying: "On the tram I saw a face such as Jesus Christ must have had in His Agony." Before going shopping he takes out the slips, riffles through them as through a pack of cards, lays them out like a game of patience, and arranges them in order of priority, forming little piles just as one separates aces, kings, queens, and jacks.

From all his books they stick halfway out between the pages, most of them yellowed and spotted because the books often lie about for months before he gets around to making use of the slips. During school holidays he collects them, rereads the passages he has made notes on, and sorts the slips, on most of which he has noted English and French words, grammatical constructions, idioms whose meaning is not fully clear to him till he has come across them two or three times. He carries on a voluminous correspondence about his discoveries, orders dictionaries to be sent to him, checks back with his colleagues, and with gentle persistence needless the editors of reference works.

And there is one slip that he always carries in his wallet, one marked in red pencil as being particularly important, a memo that is destroyed after each of my visits but is then soon written out again—the slip that says: "Have a talk with the boy!"

I recalled how surprised I had been to discover this same persistence in myself during the year I was going to the engineering school: what I knew, what I understood, never appealed to me as much as what I didn't know, what I didn't understand, and I found no peace till I could take a new machine apart and put it together again almost in my sleep; yet my curiosity was always coupled with the desire to make money out of my knowledge: a motivation that to Father would have been totally incomprehensible. The possible cost of one single word in terms of postage alone, when books have to be sent back and forth, or of trips that have to be undertaken, is of no importance to him; he loves those newly discovered words or idioms as a zoologist might love a newly discovered animal, and it would never occur to him to accept money for his discoveries.

Once again Wolf's hand lay on my shoulder, and I realized that I had risen from the running board, walked over to my car, and was looking from the outside through the windscreen at the place where

Hedwig had been sitting: how empty it was. . . .

"What's going on?" said Wolf. "What've you been doing to our nice Mrs Flink? She's terribly upset." I said nothing; Wolf kept his hand on my shoulder, pushing me past my car into Korbmacher Lane. "She phoned me," said Wolf, "and there was something in her voice that made me come right away—something that had nothing to do with her washing machines."

I said nothing. "Come on," said Wolf, "a cup of coffee is what you need."

"Yes," I said softly, "a cup of coffee is what I need," and I brushed his hand from my shoulder and went ahead of him into Korbmacher Lane, where I knew of a small café.

A young woman was just emptying some rolls from a white cloth bag into the window: the rolls piled up against the glass, and I could see their smooth brown bellies, their crisp backs, and the dazzling white on top where the baker had cut into them; they were still sliding when the young woman had turned back into the café, and for a moment they seemed to me like fish, blunt-nosed, flat fish crammed into an aquarium.

"Here?" said Wolf.

"Yes, here," I said.

Shaking his head, he went in, but smiled when I led him past the counter into the little room, which was empty.

"Not a bad place," he said, sitting down.

"No," I said, "not a bad place."

"Oh," said Wolf, "one has only to look at you to know what's the matter with you!"

"So what's the matter with me?"

"Oh," he said with a grin, "nothing. You just happen to look like someone who's already committed suicide. I can see we might as well forget about you for today."

The young woman brought the coffee ordered by Wolf at the counter.

"Father's furious," said Wolf, "the phone was ringing all through the lunch hour, no one could find you, no one could reach you, not even at the number you'd left with Mrs Brotig. Don't push him too far," said Wolf, "he's very angry. You ought to know that where business is concerned he won't stand any nonsense."

"No," I said, "where business is concerned he won't stand any nonsense."

I drank some of my coffee, stood up, went back to the counter, and asked the young woman for three rolls; she handed me a plate, and I shook my head when she offered me a knife. I put the rolls on the plate, went back into the room, sat down, and broke open a roll by placing my two thumbs side by side in the white cut and then splitting it open, and when I had eaten the first piece I could feel my nausea stop circling inside me.

"Now look," said Wolf, "surely you don't have to eat dry bread?"

"No," I said, "I don't have to."

"It's impossible to talk to you," he said.

"Yes," I said, "it's impossible to talk to me. Why don't you leave?"

"All right," he said, "maybe by tomorrow you'll be back to normal."

71

He laughed, stood up, called the woman over from the front of the café, paid for the two cups of coffee and the three rolls, but when he gave her a tip the young woman smiled and put the two coins back into his clean, capable hand, and with a shake of his head he returned them to his purse. I broke open the second roll, and I could feel Wolf's eyes as they looked at the back of my neck, my hair, and along the outline of my face down to my hands.

"By the way," he said, "we made it."

I looked up at him, puzzled.

"Didn't Ulla tell you yesterday about the Tritonia contract?"

"Yes, she did," I said softly, "she did tell me about it yesterday."

"We got the contract," said Wolf with a broad smile, "it was awarded this morning. I hope you'll have come to your senses again when we start on Friday. What do you want me to tell Father? What do I tell Father anyway? He's madder at you than he's ever been since that stupid business."

I put the roll aside and stood up.

"Since what business?" I asked. I could tell by his face that he was sorry he had mentioned it, but he had mentioned it—and I undid my hip pocket where I had put my money, slid the bills through my fingers, then remembered they were all hundreds and fifties, put the money back again, did up the button, and stuck my hand into the jacket pocket that still contained the money I had picked up again from the florist's counter. I chose a twenty-mark note, a two-mark piece, and fifty pfennigs, took Wolf's right hand, opened it, and pressed the money into it.

72

"That's for that old business," I said. "Two marks twenty-five was the price of the hot plates I swiped. Give the money to your father, there were exactly ten of them. That affair," I said softly, "must be six years old, but you and your father have never forgotten it. I'm glad you reminded me."

"I'm sorry I mentioned it," said Wolf.

"But you did mention it, right here and now—and now you've got the money, give it to your father."

"Take it back," he said, "you can't do that."

"Why not?" I asked quietly. "I stole at the time, and now I'm paying for what I stole. Anything else on the bill?"

He was silent, and now I felt sorry for him because he didn't know what to do with the money: he held it in his hand, and I could see beads of sweat forming in his cupped hand, and on his face too, and he made the kind of face he used to make when the helpers bawled him out—or when they told dirty stories.

"We were both sixteen when that business happened," I said, "we were both starting our apprenticeship—but now you're twenty-three, and you still haven't forgotten it. All right, give me back the money if it upsets you. I can send it to your father."

I opened his hand again, it was warm and moist with sweat, and I put the coins and the bill back in my pocket again.

"You'd better go now," I said softly, but he didn't move, he looked at me just as he had done all those years ago when it was found out that I had stolen: he hadn't believed it and he had defended me in his high, eager, boyish voice, and at the time—though we were less than a month apart in age—he had seemed like a much younger brother who accepts the beating the other has deserved; the old man had shouted at him and ended up by slapping him, and I would have gladly given a thousand loaves of bread not to have to admit to the theft. But I had to admit to it; out there in the yard, the workshop already in darkness, under the wretched fifteen-watt bulb dangling from a rusty socket and swinging in the November wind. Wolf's high, protesting, child's voice had been throttled by my tiny "Yes" when the old man asked me, and the two of them had gone across the yard into their apartment. Wolf had always considered me what in his childish heart he had called a "fine fellow," and it had been bitter for him to have to deprive me of this title. I felt stupid and miserable as I took the tram back to the hostel: not for a second had my conscience bothered me over the stolen hot plates that I had traded for bread and cigarettes; I had already started to worry about prices. I hadn't cared whether Wolf considered me a fine fellow or not, but I did care about him unjustly *not* considering me one.

Next morning the old man had summoned me to his office. He sent Veronika out of the room, his dark hands toyed awkwardly with his cigar, then—a thing he normally never did—he removed his green felt hat and said: "I telephoned Chaplain Derichs and just heard that you recently lost your mother. We will never mention it again, never, d'you hear? That's all."

I left the room, and when I got back to the workshop I thought: Never mention what? Mother's death? And I hated the old man more than ever: I

74

couldn't think of any reason, but I knew there was one. Since then, the matter was never mentioned again, never—and I had never stolen again, not because I might have considered stealing unjustified but because I couldn't bear for them to forgive me anything again on account of Mother's death.

"Now go," I told Wolf, "please go."

"I'm sorry," he said, "it . . . I . . ."

His eyes looked as if he still believed in fine fellows, and I said: "It's all right now, forget it and go."

He was now looking like men do who at the age of forty lose what they call their ideals: a bit puffy already and good-natured and even a bit of what they call a fine fellow.

"What do I tell Father?"

"Did he send you?"

"No," he said, "all I know is he's very angry and he'll try and get hold of you to discuss the Tritonia contract."

"I don't know yet what's going to happen."

"You really don't know?"

"No," I said, "I really don't."

"Is it true what Mrs Flink's girls are saying: that you're after a girl?"

"Yes," I said, "it's quite true what the girls are saying: I am after a girl."

"Good God, man," he said, "you oughtn't to be left alone with all that money in your pocket."

"On the contrary, I must," I said very softly, "now go, and please," I almost whispered, "don't ask me again what to tell your father."

He left, and I watched him walk past outside the window, arms hanging down like a boxer facing a

75

hopeless fight. I waited till I was sure he had turned the corner of Korbmacher Lane, then I stood in the open door and waited till I saw the Wickweber van drive off towards the station. I returned to the back room, finished my coffee standing up, and put the third roll in my pocket. I glanced at my watch, at the top part now where time was being pushed along soundlessly and slowly, and I was hoping it would be five thirty or six, but it was only four. I said good-bye to the young woman behind the counter and went back to my car: in the space between the two front seats I saw the white corner of the slip of paper I had used that morning to jot down all the customers I should have called on. I opened the door, pulled out the slip, tore it up, and threw the pieces into the gutter. What I really wanted was to return to the other side of the street and sink deep, deep down under water, but I blushed at the thought, walked to the door of Hedwig's building, and pressed the bell: I pressed twice, three times, and once more, and I waited for the sound of the buzzer, but the sound didn't come, and I pressed the bell twice more, and again the buzzer didn't sound, and the fear returned, that same fear I had felt before crossing over to Hedwig on the other side of the platform stairs—but then I heard footsteps, steps that couldn't be Mrs Grohlta's, hurried steps, down the stairs, along the corridor, and Hedwig opened the door: she was taller than I remembered, almost as tall as I am, and we were both startled to find ourselves standing so close together. She stepped back but held the door open, and I knew how heavy that door was because we had had to hold it open when we carried in the

76

washing machines for Mrs Flink till Mrs Flink had come and hooked back the door.

"There's a hook on the door," I said.

"Where?" said Hedwig.

"Here," I said, tapping the door from the outside above the doorknob, and for a few moments her left hand and her face disappeared in the dark behind the door. The light from the street fell brightly on her, and I looked at her intently; I knew it must be awful for her to be looked at like that, as if she were a picture, but her eyes held mine, she merely let her lower lip droop a little, and she looked at me as intently as I was looking at her, and I realized that my fear had left me. Once again I felt the pain this face caused within me.

"In those days," I said, "you were blonde."

"When in those days?" she asked.

"Seven years ago, just before I left home."

"Yes"—she smiled—"in those days I was blonde and anaemic."

"This morning I was on the lookout for a blonde," I told her, "and all the time you were sitting right behind me on your suitcase."

"Not for long," she said. "I had just sat down when you arrived. I recognized you right away, but I didn't want to speak to you." She smiled again.

"Why?" I asked.

"Because you looked so angry and because you seemed so grown up and important—I'm scared of important people."

"What were you thinking?" I asked.

"Oh, nothing," she said. "I was thinking: So that's young Fendrich. In the photo your father has, you

77

look much younger. They don't speak too well of you. Someone told me you had once stolen." She blushed, and I could clearly see that she was no longer anaemic: she went such a fiery red that I couldn't bear the sight.

"Don't," I said softly, "don't blush. I really did steal, but that's six years ago and it was—I'd do it again. Who told you?"

"My brother," she said, "and he's not a bad fellow at all."

"No," I said, "he's not a bad fellow at all. And you were thinking about my having stolen just now, after I had left you."

"Yes," she said, "I was, but not for long."

"How long?" I asked.

"I don't know," she said with a smile, "I was thinking about other things too. I was hungry," she went on, "but I was afraid to go downstairs because I knew you were standing here."

I took the roll out of my pocket, she accepted it with a smile, quickly broke it open, and I saw her strong white thumb sink deeply into the soft dough, as into a pillow. She ate a mouthful, and before she bit off the second I said: "You wouldn't know who told your brother about my theft?"

"Does it mean so much to you to know?"

"Yes," I said, "very much:"

"It must be the people from whom you"—she blushed—"where you did it. My brother said: 'I've had it straight from the horse's mouth.'" She bit off the second mouthful, looked past me, and said in a low voice: "I'm sorry I sent you away like that, but I was scared, and when I did it I wasn't in the least

78

thinking of what my brother had told me."

"I could almost wish," I said, "I had really stolen, but the silly thing is that it was just ineptness, nothing more. I was too young then, too scared—today I'd make a better job of it."

"You're not one bit sorry, are you?" she said, putting another piece of bread in her mouth.

"No," I said, "not one bit—only the way I got caught, that was rough, and I couldn't defend myself. And they forgave me—do you know the glorious feeling of being forgiven for something you don't feel one bit guilty about?"

"No," she said, "I don't, but I imagine it's pretty bad. You wouldn't"—she smiled—"you wouldn't happen to have some more bread in your pocket, would you? What d'you do with it? D'you feed the birds—or are you afraid of famine?"

"I'm always afraid of famine" I said. "Would you like some more?"

"Yes," she said, "I would."

"Come on then," I said, "I'll buy you some."

"Anyone would think this was a desert," she said. "I've had nothing to eat or drink for seven hours."

"Come on then," I said.

She was silent, no longer smiling. "I'll come," she said slowly, "if you promise not to come to my room again so suddenly and with so many flowers."

"I promise."

She leaned behind the door and flicked up the hook with her hand, and I heard the hook bang against the wall.

"It's not far," I said, "just round the corner, come on," but she paused, holding the closing door open with her back, waiting until I had gone ahead. I walked a little ahead of her, turning around occasionally, and it was only then that I noticed she had brought along her handbag.

Standing behind the counter in the café there was now a man slicing a fresh apple tart with a large knife: the brown pastry latticework over the green apple filling was fresh, and the man pressed the knife carefully into the tart so as not to damage the latticework. We stood side by side at the counter in silence, watching the man.

"You can get chicken broth and goulash soup here too," I told Hedwig in an undertone.

"That's right," said the man without looking up, "you can." His hair was black and thick where it came out from under his baker's cap, and he smelled of bread, the way farmers' wives smell of milk.

"No," said Hedwig, "no soup—cake."

"How much?" asked the man. He cut the last slice in the tart and jerked out the knife, smiling as he regarded his handiwork. "Want to bet," he said, his narrow, dark face crumpling up in a smile, "want to bet that all these slices are exactly the same size and weight? At most"—he laid aside the knife—"at most two or three grammes' difference, that's unavoidable. Want to bet?"

"No," I smiled, "I'm not betting; that's a bet I'd lose." The tart looked like a rose window in a cathedral. "Of course," said the man, "of course you'd lose. How much would you like?"

I looked at Hedwig. She smiled, saying: "One's not enough, and two's too much."

"One and a half, then," said the man.

"Is that possible?" she asked.

"Of course," he said; he grasped the knife and cut one of the slices exactly down the middle.

"All right then, one and a half for each of us, and some coffee."

The cups were still on the table I had sat at with Wolf, and on my plate there were still some crumbs from the rolls. Hedwig sat down on Wolf's chair, I took my cigarettes out of my pocket and held them out to her. "No thanks," she said, "maybe later."

"There's something," I said, sitting down, "I have to ask you, something I always wanted to ask your father—but of course I was too scared."

"What is it?" she said.

"Can you explain," I said, "why your name is Muller and not Müller?"

"Oh that," she said. "That's a stupid business I've often been annoyed about."

"How do you mean?" I asked.

"My grandfather was called Müller, but he made a lot of money and felt his name was too common, so he spent all kinds of money to have the two dots removed from our U. I'm furious with him."

"Why?"

"Because I'd rather be called Müller and have the money it cost to kill those two innocent little dots. I wish I had that money now, then I wouldn't have to become a teacher."

"Don't you want to?" I asked.

"It's not that I don't want to," she said, "but I'm not crazy about it. But Father says I must, so I can support myself."

"If you like," I said softly, "I'll support you."

She blushed, and I was glad I had said it at last, and had been able to say it like this. I was glad, too, that the man came in, bringing the coffee. He set the pot down on the table, removed the dirty dishes, and said: "Would you like some whipped cream on the cake?"

"Yes," I said, "some cream please."

He went off, and Hedwig poured the coffee. She was still flushed, and I looked past her at the picture hanging on the wall behind: the photograph of a marble statue of a woman. I had often driven past that monument and never known whom it represented, and it was satisfying to read now under the picture "Empress Augusta Monument", and to find out who the woman was.

The man brought the cake. I put some milk in my coffee, stirred it, broke off a piece of cake with my spoon, and was glad when Hedwig started to eat too. She was no longer flushed, and she said, without looking up from her plate: "Funny way to support me: a whole lot of flowers and a roll eaten in an open door."

"And later," I said, "cake with whipped cream and coffee—but then in the evening what my mother would have called a sensible meal."

"Yes," she said, "my mother also told me I should have something sensible to eat every day."

"Shall we say about seven?" I said.

"Tonight?" she asked.

And I said: "Yes."

"No," she said, "I can't tonight. I have to go and see a relative of Father's: she lives in a suburb, and she's been looking forward for so long to having me here."

"Are you looking forward to going?"

"No," she said. "She's one of those women who can tell at a glance when you last washed your curtains, and the worst part is: whatever she says is absolutely right. If she saw us here she'd say: 'He wants to seduce you.'"

"That's right too," I said, "I do want to seduce you."

"I know," said Hedwig, "—no, I'm not looking forward to going there."

"Then don't go," I said. "It would be nice if I could see you again tonight. One should never go to see people one doesn't like."

"All right," she said, "I won't—but if I don't go she'll come and pick me up. She has a car and is terribly forceful—no, determined is what Father always says about her."

"I hate determined people," I said.

"So do I," she said. She finished her cake and with her spoon scraped up the cream that had slid off onto the plate.

"I can't make up my mind whether to go where I ought to be going at six o'clock," I said. "I meant to meet the girl I had been intending to marry, and I meant to tell her that I don't intend to marry her." She had picked up the pot to pour out some more coffee, but she paused and said: "Does it depend on me whether you tell her today or not?"

"No," I said, "only on me, I'll have to tell her in any case."

"Then go there and tell her. Who is she?"

"She's the one," I said, "whose father I stole from,

and probably the one who told whoever it was who told your brother."

"Oh," she said, "then that must make it easy for you."

"Too easy," I said. "So easy it's almost like cancelling a newspaper subscription when you're not sorry for the newspaper but only for the person who delivers it, who will now get one tip less every month."

"Go and see her," she said, "and I won't go to that relative of Father's. When d'you have to leave?"

"Around six," I said, "but it's not yet five."

"Leave me here," said Hedwig, "go and look for a stationer's and buy me a postcard: I promised the family to write every day."

"Would you like some more coffee?" I asked.

"No thanks," she said, "but you can give me a cigarette."

I held out the packet, she took a cigarette. I lit it for her, and as I stood at the counter to pay I could still see her sitting there smoking. I could tell she didn't smoke very often, I could tell by the way she held her cigarette and puffed out the smoke, and when I went back again into the room she glanced up and said: "Why don't you go?" so I left again and just caught a glimpse of her opening her handbag: the lining was as green as her coat.

I walked the whole length of Korbmacher Lane, turned the corner into Netzmacher Lane; it had got chilly, and the lights were on in some of the windows. I had to walk all along Netzmacher Lane before finding a stationer's.

On the old-fashioned shelves inside, everything

84

was piled up or lying around in disorder; on the counter was a pack of cards that someone had obviously looked through and rejected, he had laid the defective cards beside the opened package, an ace of diamonds on which the big diamond in the middle had faded, and a nine of spades with a bent corner. There were also some ball-point pens lying around, next to a pad used by someone to try them out. I leaned on the counter and looked at the pad. There were squiggles on it, rapid whorls, someone had written "Bruno Street", but most people had tried out their signature, the first letter revealing the little effort made by each person. "Maria Kählisch", clearly written in a firm round hand, and someone else had written like a stutterer: "Robert B- - Robert Br- - Robert Brach" it read, the writing angular, old-fashioned, and touching, I felt it must have been an old man. Somebody had written "Heinrich", and then in the same handwriting "Forget-me-not", and a person using a thick pen had scrawled: "What a dump."

At last a young woman appeared who gave me a friendly nod and put the pack of cards with the two defective cards back in its case.

First I asked for some postcards, five; from the pile she placed in front of me I took the top five: they were scenes of parks and churches and one of a monument I had never seen: it was called the Noldewohl Monument and showed a man in bronze wearing a frock coat and holding a scroll he was in the act of unrolling.

"Who do you suppose Noldewohl was?" I asked the young woman, handing her the card, which she put into the envelope with the others. She had a very good-natured red face, wore her dark hair parted in the middle, and looked as women do who intend to enter a convent.

"Noldewohl," she said, "was the man who built the North Town."

I knew the North Town. Tall apartment blocks still trying to maintain the good middle-class standards of 1910; trams curved along the streets, wide green cars that to me looked as romantic as a stagecoach would have seemed to my father in 1910.

"Thanks," I said, and I thought: So that's what used to get you a monument.

"Would there be anything else?" asked the woman, and I said: "Yes, would you mind getting out that box of writing paper, the big green one?"

She opened the display case, took out the box, and blew the dust off it.

I watched her pull some wrapping paper off a roll hanging on the wall behind, and I admired her pretty pale little hands, and on an impulse I took my fountain pen out of my pocket, unscrewed the cap, and wrote my name under "Maria Kählisch" on the pad used by people to try out ball-points. I don't know why I did it, but I felt such an urge to be immortalized on that piece of paper.

"Oh," said the woman, "did you want your pen filled?"

"No," I said, and I could feel myself blushing, "no thank you, it's just been filled."

She smiled, and it almost seemed as if she knew why I had done it.

86

I put some money on the counter, took my chequebook from my breast pocket, and on the counter made out a cheque for twenty-two marks fifty, writing across it "For Deposit Only", took the envelope the woman had used for the postcards, stuffed the cards into my pocket, and put the cheque into the envelope. It was the cheapest kind of envelope, like the ones you get from the tax office or the police. As I wrote Wickweber's address the ink ran, and I crossed it out and rewrote it, slowly.

From the change that the woman had pushed towards me, I took one mark, pushed it back, and said to her: "Could you let me have some stamps, ten-pfennig ones and some charity ones?" She opened a drawer, took some stamps out of a booklet, and handed them to me, and I stuck two on the envelope.

I felt the urge to spend some more money, left the change lying on the counter, and looked around for something on the shelves; there were some student's notebooks, the kind we had used in engineering school: I chose one bound in soft green leather and handed it across the counter for the woman to wrap, and again she spun the roll of wrapping paper—and I knew, as soon as I took the parcel, that Hedwig would never use that notebook for her lectures.

As I walked back through Netzmacher Lane it seemed as if this day would never end: the lights in the shop windows were merely shining a bit brighter. I would have been glad to spend some more money, but nothing in any of the windows made me want to buy; the only place where I paused was in front of a coffinmaker's—I stood looking at the boxes, dark brown and black, under their feeble lighting, then walked on and thought of Ulla as I turned back into Korbmacher Lane. It wasn't going to be all that easy, I realized: she had known me a long time, and she knew me well, but I knew her too. When I kissed her, I had sometimes seen beneath the smooth, pretty girl's face the empty skull her father would one day have: an empty skull wearing a green felt hat.

Together she and I had cheated the old man, by a method more cunning and profitable than the one I had used for the hot plates: we had made more money, and good money, by selling some of the scrap metal I salvaged, with the aid of a whole crew of workmen, from ruins that were slated for demolition. Many of the rooms we reached by long ladders had been completely intact, we had found bathrooms and kitchens where every range, every boiler, every screw, was as good as new, every enamel hook, hooks with towels still hanging on them, glass shelves still holding lipstick and razor side by side, bathtubs still full of bath water where the suds had sunk to the bottom in chalky flakes, clear water with rubber toys still floating in it, toys played with by children before they suffocated in the cellar, and I had gazed into mirrors in which people had looked a few minutes before they died, mirrors in which, filled with rage and disgust, I shattered my own face with a hammer—silver splinters fell over razor and lipstick. I pulled the plug out of the bathtub, the water fell four floors down, and the rubber animals sank slowly to the chalky bottom of the tub.

In one place there had been a sewing machine, its

88

needle still stuck in the piece of brown cloth that was to have become a pair of boy's shorts, and no one understood me when I tipped it through the open door, past the ladder, down to where it shattered on rubble and collapsed walls; but what satisfied me most was destroying my own face in the mirrors we found—the silver splinters falling like a tinkling fluid. Till Wickweber began to wonder why no mirrors ever turned up in the loot—and one of the other helpers was put in charge of the salvaging.

But I was the one they sent when the apprentice fell to his death. He had climbed into a ruined building one night to remove an automatic washing machine: no one could explain how he had got to the third floor, but he had, and he had tried to let down the machine, the size of a bedside table, on a rope, and had been yanked down by the weight. His handcart was still standing in the sunshine down on the street when we arrived. The police were there, and someone was measuring the length of the rope with a tape measure, shaking his head, looking up to where the kitchen door still stood open and you could see a broom propped against the pale-blue wall. The washing machine had cracked open like a nut: the drum had rolled out, but the boy lay there with no sign of injury, he had plunged into a pile of rotting mattresses, lay buried in dried seaweed, and his mouth was as bitter as ever: the mouth of a hungry creature who had no faith in the justice of this world. His name was Alois Fruklahr, and he had been no more than three days at Wickweber's. I carried him to the hearse, and a woman standing on the street asked: "Was he your brother?" And I said: "Yes, he

89

was my brother'"—and that afternoon I saw Ulla dipping her pen in red ink and crossing his name off the payroll with a ruler: it was a straight, neat stroke, and it was as red as blood, as red as Scharnhorst's collar, as Iphigenia's lips, as the heart on the ace of hearts.

Hedwig had been cupping her head in her hands, the sleeves of her green pullover had slipped down, and her firm white forearms stood solidly on the table like bottles, her face wedged between their necks and filling the curve between the tapering bottlenecks; her eyes were dark brown, with an undertone of pale yellow, almost honey-coloured, and I saw my shadow fall into them. But she continued to look past me: she was looking into that corridor that I had walked along exactly twelve times, carrying the modern-language journals, the corridor I had only a vague, dim memory of: reddish linoleum—but it may also have been dark brown, for there wasn't much light in that corridor; the photo of her father wearing his student's cap and with the elaborate insignia of some Onia or other—the smell of peppermint tea, of tobacco—and a music shelf on which I had once been able to read the title on the top sheet: Grieg—"Anitra's Dance".

I now wished I had known that corridor as intimately as she did, and I searched my memory for objects I might have forgotten: I slit open my memory the way you slit open a coat lining to remove the coin you have felt in there—a coin that suddenly becomes infinitely precious because it's the last, the only one: the ten pfennigs for two rolls, for a cigarette, or for a small tube of peppermints whose white tablets, shaped like a Communion wafer, can fill hunger with their spicy sweetness just as the lung that no longer functions can be pumped full of air.

There is dust in your hand after the lining has been slit open, woollen fluff, and the finger digs around for the precious coin that you know is ten pfennigs but that you now begin to hope is a mark. But it was only ten pfennigs, I had found it, and it was precious: over the front door—I had always seen it on leaving and not before—there had hung a picture of the Sacred Heart, with an oil lamp in front of it.

"You'd better go now," said Hedwig. "I'll wait for you here. Will you be long?" She spoke without looking at me.

"This place closes at seven," I said.

"Will you be later than seven?"

"No," I said, "I'm sure I won't. Will you be here?"

"Yes," she said, "I'll be here. You'd better go."

I put the postcards on the table, the stamps beside them, and went—went back to Juden Lane, got into my car, threw the two parcels containing Hedwig's presents on the back seat. I realized that all the time I had been scared of my car, the same way I was scared of my work; but the driving went without a hitch, just as smoking a cigarette had gone without a hitch while I stood on the other side of the street and looked across at the doorway. The driving went automatically: there were knobs to press, knobs to pull, levers to press down, levers to pull up. I drove as one drives in a dream: it went smoothly, quietly, and with precision, and I felt as if I were driving through a soundless world.

As I drove across the intersection of Juden Lane

and Korbmacher Lane, in the direction of Röntgen Square, I saw Hedwig's green pullover disappear in the dusk at the bottom of Korbmacher Lane and, in the middle of the intersection, I turned and drove after her. She was running, then she spoke to a man crossing the street carrying a loaf of bread under his arm. I stopped, because I was so close, and I could see the man explaining something to her with gestures. Hedwig ran on, and I slowly followed her as she ran partway along Netzmacher Lane, and then turned beyond the stationer's where I had bought the postcards into a short, dark street I didn't know. She wasn't running now, her black bag dangled from her hand, and for an instant I switched on the high beam so as to see to the end of the street, and then I blushed with shame as my headlight fell full on the doorway to a little church Hedwig was just entering. I felt like a person must feel who is making a film, suddenly cutting the night in two with his spotlight and catching a couple in an embrace.

PART THREE

I DROVE quickly around the church, turned the car, and drove to Röntgen Square. I arrived there on the dot of six and could see Ulla waiting outside the butcher's as I turned from Tschlandler Street into the square: I saw her all the time while, boxed in by other cars, I crawled around Röntgen Square till at last I could find a place to park. She had on her red coat and black hat, and I recalled having once told her how much I liked her in that red coat. I left the car at the curb, and as I hurried towards her the first thing she said was: "You can't park there. It might cost you twenty marks."

I could tell from her face that she had already talked to Wolf, there were dark shadows over the rosy skin. Between two white blocks of lard at the back of the butcher's window, above her head, between some flower vases and marble slabs, stood a pyramid of canned meat, with labels printed in garish red: "Corned Beef".

"Never mind the car," I said. "We haven't got much time."

"Nonsense," she said, "give me the key. There's a space over there now."

I handed her the key and watched her get into my car and manoeuvre it skilfully from the prohibited to the other side, where another car had just driven off. Then I walked to the postbox at the corner and posted the letter to her father.

"What nonsense," she said as she returned and handed me the key. "As if you had money to throw away."

I sighed and thought of the endlessness of the long, lifelong marriage that I had almost shared with her; of the reproaches that would have dropped into me in the course of thirty, forty years, like stones dropping into a well; how surprised she would have been if the echo of the falling stones had grown fainter, duller, short—till she heard no echo at all and the stones had grown up out of the well, and the vision of a well vomiting stones pursued me as I walked with her around the corner to Café Joos.

I said: "Have you been talking to Wolf?" And she said: "Yes." And I grasped her arm as we stood in front of Café Joos and asked: "Is there any more to be said?"

"Oh yes," she replied. "There's lots more to be said."

She pushed me into the café, and as I drew aside the baize curtain I knew why she was so eager to sit here with me. This was where I had so often come with her and Wolf, even in the days when I was still going to night school with Wolf, and later too, when we had graduated and weren't going to engineering school any more, Café Joos had been our meeting place: together we had drunk countless cups of coffee, eaten countless portions of ice cream, and when I saw Ulla's smile as she stood beside me looking around for a vacant table I knew she thought she had lured me into a trap: here the walls, the tables, the chairs, the smells, even the faces of the waitresses—they were all on her side; here she would do battle with me on ground where the stage setting was her stage setting, but what she didn't know was that those years—it must have been three or four—were erased from my memory, though I had been sitting here with her as recently as yesterday. I had tossed out the years as one tosses out a souvenir which, at the moment of acquisition, had seemed so valuable and significant: the piece of rock picked up on the summit of Mont Blanc as a memento of the instant when one suddenly knew the meaning of: He felt giddy—that chip of grey stone, the size of a matchbox, that looks just like billions of tons of rock on this earth, that one suddenly drops out of the train window between the rails, where it mingles with the crushed stone.

The previous evening we had been there till quite late; she had picked me up after evening Mass, and back in the gents of the café I had washed my hands, still dirty from work; I had had a meat pie, some wine—and somewhere in my trouser pocket, pushed down by my money, must still be the receipt given me by the waitress. Six marks fifty-eight must be the amount on it, and I could see the girl who had given it to me hanging the evening newspapers on a rack at the far end.

"Shall we sit down?" asked Ulla.

"O.K.," I said, "let's."

Mrs Joos was standing behind the counter, arranging chocolates in glass dishes with silver tongs. I had hoped we could avoid being greeted by her; she set great store by this, having what she called "a soft spot for young people"—but here she was, emerging from behind the counter, holding out both hands and clasping my wrists since I was carrying my car key in one hand and my hat in the other, and she exclaimed: "How nice to see you again so soon!" and I felt myself blushing and looked in embarrassment into those attractive almond-shaped eyes that told me how attractive I am to women. Through her daily association with chocolates, whose custodian she is, Mrs Joos has grown to resemble them; she looks like a chocolate: sweet, neat, appetizing, and her dainty fingers are always slightly spread from handling the silver tongs. She is small and hops around like a little bird, and the two strands of white hair running back from her temples always remind me of certain marzipan stripes on certain chocolates. Her head, that narrow, oval cranium, contains the entire chocolate-topography of the town: she knows exactly which woman prefers which chocolates, which varieties will please which person—and so she is every beau's adviser, the trusted consultant of those large companies that on festive occasions shower little gifts on the wives of important customers. Which adulteries are pending, which have already occurred, is clear to her from the consumption of certain assortments of chocolates; also, she creates new assortments and cleverly sees to it that these quickly become the fashion.

She shook hands with Ulla and smiled at her; I put the car key back in my pocket, and she released Ulla and shook hands with me again.

I looked more closely into those attractive eyes and tried to imagine what she would have said had I come here seven years ago and asked for some bread—and I saw those eyes get narrower still, hard and dry like those of a goose, and I saw those charming, daintily spread fingers contract like claws, saw that soft, manicured hand grow wrinkled and yellow with greed, and I withdrew my own so abruptly that she was startled and shook her head as she went back behind her counter, and now her face looked like a chocolate that has fallen in the dirt, its centre oozing into the gutter, not a sweet centre but a sour one.

Ulla drew me away, and we walked past the occupied tables along the rust-red carpet towards the back of the café, where she must have spotted two empty chairs. There was no vacant table, just those two chairs at a table for three. A man was sitting there with a cigar in his mouth, reading a newspaper; as he exhaled, wisps of pale-grey smoke came out at the tip through the ash, and tiny ash particles fell onto his dark suit.

"Here?" I said.

"There's nothing else free," said Ulla.

"Don't you think," I said, "we'd better go to another café?"

She threw a venomous glance at the man, looked around, and I noticed the triumphant gleam in her eyes as a man stood up in the corner to help his wife on with her pale-blue coat. For her—I felt it again as I followed her—for her it was unutterably important that our talk should take place here. She threw her bag onto the chair, on which a shoebox belonging to the woman in the blue coat was still lying—and the woman in the blue coat shook her head as she picked up her box and followed her husband, who was standing between the tables paying the waitress.

Ulla pushed the dirty dishes to one side and sat down on the chair in the corner. I sat down next to her, took my cigarettes out of my pocket, and held them out to her; she took one, I lit it for her, also one for myself; I looked at the dirty plates with bits of icing smeared on them, cherry stones sticking to them, looked at the grey, milky remains in one of the coffee cups.

"I should have known," said Ulla, "when I used to watch you through the glass partition that divided the accounting office from the factory. The way you carried on with those factory girls just to get a bite of their sandwich: there was one kid, an ugly little thing, one of the armature-winders, she must have had rickets, she had a grey, pimply face—she gave you half her jam sandwich, and I watched you stuff it into your mouth."

"What you don't know is that I kissed her too, and took her to the movies and held her hand in the dark; and that she died just at the time I was taking my journeyman's test. And that I spent a whole week's wages on flowers for her grave. I hope she's forgiven me for that half-sandwich."

Ulla looked at me in silence, then pushed the dirty

100

dishes still farther away, and I pushed them back again because one plate had almost fallen onto the floor.

"Your family," I said, "didn't even bother to send a wreath to her funeral; not so much as a condolence card to her parents. I assume all you did was cross her name off the payroll with a neat, straight stroke in red ink."

The waitress came, cleared the plates and cups onto a tray, and asked: "Two coffees?"

"No thanks," I said, "not for me."

"But I'll have one," said Ulla.

"And for you?" the girl turned to me.

"Anything will do," I said listlessly.

"Suppose you bring Mr Fendrich some peppermint tea," Ulla said.

"Yes," I said, "that'll do."

"Oh dear," said the waitress, "we haven't any peppermint tea, I'm afraid, but we do have Indian."

"Yes, Indian will do," I said, and the waitress went off.

I looked at Ulla and was amazed, as I had so often been, to see those full, pretty lips become as narrow and thin as the lines she drew with her ruler.

I took off my wristwatch and laid it beside me on the table; it was ten past six, and I meant to leave not a minute later than a quarter to seven.

"I would have gladly paid the twenty marks to have two minutes longer to talk to you, I'd have gladly given you those two minutes as a farewell present, like two precious flowers—but you've robbed yourself of them. For me those two minutes were worth twenty marks."

101

"Yes," she said, "you're living in grand style all right, giving away flowers at ten marks apiece."

"Yes," I said, "it seemed worth it to me, seeing we've never given each other anything. Never, have we?"

"No," she said, "we never have. I was taught that presents have to be earned—and I've never felt you had earned one, and I don't ever seem to have earned one either."

"No," I said, "and the only thing I've ever wanted to give you, though you hadn't earned it, that one gift you wouldn't accept. And every time we went out together"—I dropped my voice—"we never forgot to get a receipt for income tax, alternately for the firm and for me. And if there were such things as receipts for kisses, then I'm sure you'd have them all in a file."

"There are such things as receipts for kisses," she said, "and one day you'll see for yourself."

The waitress came with Ulla's coffee and my tea, and the whole ceremony seemed to take forever: this arranging of plates, cups, milk jugs, sugar pots, the holder for the teabag, and there was even a tiny dish for the silver pincers that held a sliver of lemon in its teeth.

Ulla was silent, and I was afraid she was going to scream; I had heard her screaming once, when her father refused to appoint her a signatory for the firm. Time stood still; it was thirteen minutes past six.

"Damn," said Ulla under her breath. "You might at least put your watch away."

I covered the watch with the menu.

I felt as if I had been forced to see, hear, and smell

all of this countless times, like the record put on every evening at a certain time by the people living above me—like a film shown in Hell: always the same one, and this smell in the air, of coffee, of sweat, perfume, liqueurs, and cigarettes: what I was saying—what Ulla was saying—it had all been said countless times, and it was all wrong, the words had a false taste on the tongue; it reminded me of what I had told Father about the black market and about my hunger: as the words came out they ceased to be true—and suddenly I recalled the scene when Helene Frenkel had given me her jam sandwich, so vividly that I seemed to taste the cheap red jam, and I longed for Hedwig and for the dark-green shadow of the bridge where Jürgen Brolaski had vanished.

"I can't *quite* see it," said Ulla, "because I can't see there being some things you don't do for money—or has she got money?"

"No," I said, "she hasn't got money—but she knows that I once stole; one of you must have told somebody who told her brother. Wolf has just reminded me about it too."

"Yes," she said, "and a good thing he did: you've become such a snob, you were probably beginning to forget that you once stole some hot plates to buy cigarettes."

"And bread," I said, "the bread that you, that your father, never gave me—only Wolf sometimes gave me some. He never knew the meaning of hunger, but he always gave me his bread when we worked together. I believe," I went on in a low voice, "that if in those days you had just once given me a loaf of bread, I couldn't possibly be sitting here

103

talking to you like this."

"The wages we paid were always higher than the standard scale, and everyone working at the plant got a living allowance and some ration-free soup at midday."

"That's right," I said. "The wages you paid were always higher than the standard rate, and everyone working at the plant got a living allowance and some ration-free soup at midday."

"You bastard," she said, "you ungrateful bastard."

I lifted the menu off my watch, but it wasn't yet six thirty, so I laid the menu back over the watch.

"Examine the payrolls again," I said, "payrolls you kept. Read the names again—out loud, reverently, like you'd read a litany—call them out, and after each name say 'Forgive us'—then add up all the names, multiply the number by a thousand loaves of bread—and that result again by a thousand: then you'll have the number of curses heaped on your father's bank account. The unit is bread, the bread of those early years, years that lie in my memory as if under a dense fog: the soup that was doled out to us slopped around feebly in our stomachs, it would rise in us, hot and sour, as we rode home in the evening on the swaying tramcar: it was the belch of impotence, and the only pleasure we had was hatred—hatred," I said softly, "—that has long since flown out of me like a belch that's been pressing hard against my stomach. Oh, Ulla," I whispered, looking at her directly for the first time. "Are you really trying to persuade me, to make me believe, that the soup and the little extra allowance were enough—is that what you're trying to do? Just remember those big rolls of oil paper!"

She stirred her coffee, looked at me again, and held out her cigarettes: I took one, gave her a light, and lit my own.

"I don't even mind you and your family telling other people about that legendary theft of mine—but are you seriously trying to make me believe that all of us, every single person on your payroll, didn't occasionally deserve an extra loaf or two of bread?"

She remained silent, staring past me, and I said: "In those days, when I lived at home, I used to steal books from my father to buy myself bread—books he loved, that he had collected, that he'd gone hungry for as a student—books for which he'd paid the price of twenty loaves of bread and I sold for the price of half a loaf: that's the interest we got—minus two hundred to minus infinity."

"We pay interest too," said Ulla quietly, "—interest you know nothing about."

"Yes," I said, "you do pay interest, and you don't even know how high the percentage is—but I, I took those books at random, choosing them only for size. My father had so many, I thought he'd never notice—it was much later that I realized he knows every single one of them as well as a shepherd knows his flock—and one of those books was quite small and shabby, nothing to look at—I sold it for the price of a box of matches—but later I found out it was worth a whole cartload of bread. Later my father asked me, blushing as he did so, to leave the selling of his books to him—and he sold them himself, sending me the money, and I bought bread. . . ."

She winced as I said "bread", and now I felt sorry for her. "Slap me if you like," she said, "throw the tea in my face—talk, go on talking, you who never wanted to talk—but please don't say the word 'bread' again, spare me the sound of it—please."

And I said softly: "I'm sorry—I won't say it any more." I looked at her again and was shocked: the Ulla who was sitting there was changing under my very words, under my very eyes, under the effect of the little watch hand that was grinding away under the menu: she was no longer the one for whom my words had been meant. I had imagined she would talk a lot and be right in some way that didn't matter—but now I had talked a lot, and I was the one who was right in a way that didn't matter.

She looked at me, and I knew that later, when she was walking past the dark workshop into her father's house, between the shrubs bordering the gravel path, under the elderberry tree: that she would do what I would have least expected of her: she would weep, and a weeping Ulla was a person I didn't know.

I had imagined she would emerge the winner, but now I was the winner, and I could feel the sour taste of that victory on my tongue.

She had not touched her coffee, she was toying with her spoon, and her voice startled me when she spoke: "I'd gladly give you a blank cheque for you to withdraw the curses from our bank account. It's nice to know that you've been thinking about these things all these years, counting the curses, without telling me."

106

"I haven't been thinking about it all these years," I said, "it's not like that: today, maybe here for the first time, I remembered: you pour red dye into a spring to find out how far it reaches, but it may be years before you find the dyed water somewhere you didn't expect to. Today the streams are running blood, today for the first time I know where my red dye went."

"You may be right," she said. "It's the same with me—today, now, for the first time I know that money isn't important to me: I wouldn't mind giving a second blank cheque plus a bank statement, and you could withdraw as much as you wanted, and it wouldn't bother me—and I've always thought it would bother me. Maybe you're right—but it's all too late."

"Yes," I said, "it's too late—you see the horse you'd wanted to bet a thousand marks on coming in first—the betting slip's already in your hand, all filled out, that slip of paper that would be worth a fortune if you'd placed the bet, but you didn't, and the slip is worthless, there's no point in keeping it as a souvenir."

"All that's left is the thousand marks," she said, "but *you* would probably throw the thousand marks along with the betting slip into the gutter."

"Yes," I said, "that's probably what I'd do." I poured some milk into the cold tea, squeezed the lemon into it, and watched the milk curdle and sink to the bottom in yellowish-grey flakes. I offered my cigarettes to Ulla, but she shook her head, and I didn't feel like smoking either and put the packet away. I lifted the menu slightly from my watch, saw it was ten minutes to seven, and quickly replaced the menu over the watch, but she had noticed and said: "You'd better go—I'll stay here."

"Can't I drive you home?" I asked.

"No," she said, "I'll stay here. You'd better go now."

But I didn't get up, and she said: "This is good-bye," and I held out my hand. She clasped it for a moment without looking at it, then suddenly dropped it before I had time to think she would let go, and my hand struck the edge of the table.

"I'm sorry," she said, "I didn't mean to do that." I felt a sharp pain in my hand, but I believed her when she said she hadn't done it deliberately.

"I've often watched your hands, the way they held a tool, the way they handled an appliance—the way you took apart appliances you knew nothing about, examined the way they worked, and put them together again. Anyone could see you were born for this job, that you love it—and that it was better to let you earn your bread that way than just to give it to you."

"I don't love it," I said. "I hate it, the way a boxer hates boxing."

"You must go now," she said, "go on," and I left, without another word, without looking back, till I reached the counter; then I walked back and, standing between the tables, paid the waitress for the coffee and the tea.

PART FOUR

It was dark, still Monday, as I drove back to Juden Lane; I drove fast. But it was already seven o'clock, I had forgotten that the Nudelbreite is closed to traffic after seven, and I found myself driving round it in circles through dark streets where there were no buildings, emerging again at the church where I had last seen Hedwig.

It struck me that both Hedwig and Ulla had told me to "go, go".

I drove once more past the stationer's, the coffin-maker's in Korbmacher Lane, and I was dismayed to see that there was no longer a light in the café. I was about to drive past, into Juden Lane, when I glimpsed Hedwig's green pullover at the entrance to the café, and I jammed on my brakes so hard that the car skidded and slid across the muddy strip where the street had been torn up and filled in again, and my left hand banged against the door

111

handle. Both hands were hurting as I got out and walked towards Hedwig in the dark; she was standing there like the girls who had sometimes accosted me when I was walking along a dark street at night: without a coat, in her bright-green pullover, her white face beneath her dark hair, and still whiter—painfully white—her neck in the small, leaf-shaped opening; and her lips looked as though they had been drawn in black ink.

She did not move, did not speak or look at me, and without a word I took her hand and pulled her towards the car.

A small crowd had gathered, the sound of my brakes having swept through the silent street like a tumpet blast, and I jerked open the door, almost pushed Hedwig inside, hastened around to the other side, and drove off in a hurry. Not until a minute later, when we were way beyond the station, did I have time to look at her. She was deathly pale, holding her body as straight as a statue.

I pulled up under a streetlamp. It was a dark street, and the circle of light fell onto a park, cutting a round piece of grass out of the darkness; it was silent all around.

"A man accosted me," said Hedwig, startling me because she was still looking straight ahead like a statue, "a man. He wanted to take me along or go along with me, and he looked so nice. He had a brief-case under his arm, and his teeth were slightly yellow from smoking; he was old, at least thirty-five, but he was nice."

"Hedwig," I said, but she didn't look at me, until I took her arm, and then she turned her head and said

112

softly: "Drive me home, Walter"—and I was moved by the natural way in which she used my first name.

"I'll drive you home," I said. "Oh Christ."

"No, let's stay here for a moment," she said. And she looked at me, looked at me closely, as closely as I had once looked at her, but now I dared not look at her. I broke out in a sweat, and I felt the pain in both hands—and that day, that Monday, seemed unbearably long, too long for a single day, and I knew I should never have left her room: I had discovered the new land and still had not planted my flag. The land was beautiful, but it was strange too, as strange as it was beautiful.

"Oh God," she whispered, "I'm so glad you're nicer than he is. Much nicer, the baker wasn't nearly as nice as he looked. At seven o'clock sharp he kicked me out. You shouldn't have been late. Let's drive on now," she said. I drove slowly, and the dark streets I drove along seemed like trails across a swamp the car could sink into at any moment; I drove carefully, as if I had a load of explosives, and I heard her voice, was aware of her hand on my arm, and felt almost like someone who has passed the great test on Judgment Day.

"I very nearly did go with him," she was saying. "I don't know how long he would have had to keep trying, but he didn't try too long. He wanted to marry me, wanted to get a divorce—and he had children, and he was nice; but he ran off as soon as your headlights lit up the street. It was only a minute that he stood there with me, whispering hurriedly like people who don't have much time—and he didn't have much time: one minute, and I lived a whole lifetime at his side in that minute: I fell into his arms, out of his arms again; I bore his children, I darned his socks, in the evening when he came home I took his briefcase, kissed him when the front door had closed behind him; I shared his pleasure in his new set of teeth—and when he got a rise we had a little celebration: there was cake and we went to the cinema, and he bought me a new hat, as red as cherry jam; he did with me what you wanted to do with me, and I liked his clumsy caresses—I saw him swap his suits around, turning his best suit into an everyday one when he got a new best suit—then that one was demoted too—he got another new suit, and the children grew up, wore hats as red as cherry jam, and I forbade them to do what I was always forbidden to do: go for walks in the rain. I forbade them for the same reason I was forbidden: because clothes are so quickly ruined in the rain. . . . I was his widow, and received a letter of condolence from the firm. He was a cost accountant in a chocolate factory—and in the evening he would divulge how much profit his firm made on their 'Jussupoff' chocolates; they made a huge profit—and he told me to keep quiet about it, but I didn't; when I was buying milk the next morning I blurted out how much profit his firm made on their 'Jussupoff' chocolates. He need only have kept on trying for another minute or two, but he didn't: he ran, ran like a hare when your car turned into the street. 'I do have some education, miss,' he told me.''

I drove even slower, for my left hand ached badly and my right was beginning to swell a little; I drove into Juden Lane as slowly as if I were driving across a bridge that might collapse.

114

"Why did you come this way?" Hedwig asked. "Do you want to stop here?"

I looked at her as nervously as the man must have looked at her.

"We can't go to my room," she said. "Hilde Kamenz is there waiting for me. I've seen a light in my room and her car outside the door."

I drove slowly past the door, that brown door whose image I would see again when it came out of the darkroom: sheet upon sheet of doors—stacks of sheets of doors, like stacks of new stamps leaving the government printing office.

A maroon car was parked in front of this door.

I looked at Hedwig questioningly.

"Hilde Kamenz," she said, "is that relative of Father's. Drive round the corner; from my window I could see a vacant lot in the side street: I saw the dark pavement there, with the brown muddy strip in the middle, and I saw you lying there dead, for I was afraid you'd never come back."

I turned the car and drove into Korbmacher Lane, so slowly that I felt as if I could never again drive fast. A few buildings beyond the bakery was the vacant lot, and we were looking at the back of the building where Hedwig lived: the tall trees hid part of it, but we could see a whole vertical row of windows: on the ground floor the window was dark, on the second floor the light was on, and the window on the third floor was lit up too.

"My room," she said. "If she opened the window we could see her silhouette: you would have walked blindly into the trap—she'd have dragged us off to her apartment, a wonderful apartment, beautiful as

115

apartments are that owe their beauty to mere chance—but one look is enough to tell you that the 'chance' is just a matter of skilful arrangement, and it's like when you come out of a cinema and you're all wrought up by the film and then somebody coming out through the lobby says: 'Not a bad film, but the music was only so-so?' There she is!"

I looked away from Hedwig up to her room again and saw the silhouette of a woman wearing a pointed hat, and though I couldn't make out her eyes I felt sure she was looking at our car with the eyes of a woman who wants to bring order into the lives of other people.

"Drive to your place," Hedwig said, "right now. I'm so scared she'll recognize us down here, and if we fall into her hands we'll spend the entire evening in her apartment drinking her excellent tea and without even the hope that the kids will wake up and distract her. Those kids, you see, are brought up according to the book; they sleep from seven at night till seven in the morning. Come on!—and her husband's not even there either, he's out of town. Somewhere he's being paid a large fee to decorate other people's apartments to look as though they owed their beauty to mere chance. Let's go!"

Off I drove, along Korbmacher and Netzmacher Lane, slowly crossed the Nudelbreite, let myself cruise around Röntgen Square, glanced into the window of the butcher's shop, still with its pyramid of corned beef, and once again I thought of Ulla and the years with her: those years had shrunk, like a shirt that hasn't stood up to the laundry—but the time since noon, since Hedwig's arrival, was a different time.

I was tired, and my eyes smarted, and as I drove down that long, straight Münchner Road I found myself almost alone on the right-hand side while to my left oncoming cars were crowding one another and passing each other, blaring their horns and screeching past one another in triumph: there must have been some boxing event or bicycle race at the stadium, I was in the constant glare of the headlights of oncoming cars; their light dazzled me, the stabbing pain in my eyes made me groan; it was like running the gauntlet of an endless row of long flashing spears, each one piercing me and tormenting me with its light. I felt scourged with light—and I was reminded of the years when I woke up in the mornings and hated the light: for two years I had felt the urge to get ahead, and every morning I had got up at five thirty, drunk a cup of bitter tea, wrestled with formulas, or gone down to my little basement workshop to tinker, file, and assemble, to test models that often overloaded the building's wiring so that the fuses blew and I could hear indignant voices upstairs shouting about the water for their coffee. The alarm clock had stood beside me on my desk or on the workbench, and only when it rang, at eight o'clock, would I go upstairs, shower, and go into my landlady's kitchen to get my breakfast—I had been working for two and a half hours before most people had begun their breakfast. I had hated those two and a half hours, sometimes I had loved them too, but I had never permitted myself to miss them. And then, while at breakfast in my sunny room, I had often felt this scourge of light, just as I was feeling it now.

The Müncher Road was very long, and I was glad to have left the stadium behind us.

Hedwig hesitated, she hesitated only for an instant when we stopped: I held the car door open for her, helped her out, and staggered up the stairs ahead of her.

It was seven thirty, and I felt that Eternity must be a Monday: it had been less than eleven hours since I had left the house.

I listened for sounds from the corridor, heard my landlady's children laughing at the supper table, and I saw now why my feet had been so heavy as I walked up the stairs: lumps of mud clung to my shoes, and Hedwig's shoes were muddy too, from the trench down the middle of Korbmacher Lane.

"I won't turn on the light," I said to Hedwig as we went into my room. My eyes were too sore.

"No," she said, "don't turn it on," and I shut the door behind her.

A subdued light fell into the room from the windows of the building across the street, and on the desk I could see the messages Mrs Brotig had jotted down for me. The slips of paper were weighted down by a stone; I picked up the stone, weighed it in my hand like a missile, opened the window, and tossed it into the front yard: I could hear it roll across the lawn in the dark and strike the dustbin. I left the window, counted the messages in the dark: there were seven, and I tore them up and threw the pieces into the wastebasket.

"Is there any soap?" Hedwig asked behind me. "I'd like to wash my hands, the water in my room was all rusty and dirty."

"The soap's on the left, on the lower shelf," I said.

I took a cigarette from the packet, lit it, and when I turned to blow out the match and toss it into the ashtray I saw Hedwig's face in the mirror: her lips looked like the ones printed on the squares of paper I used for drying my razor blades—there was the sound of running water, she was washing her hands; I heard her rubbing them together. I was waiting for something, and I knew what I had been waiting for when there was a gentle tap at my door. It was my landlady, and I quickly went to the door, opened it a little, and slipped out into the corridor.

She was just untying her apron, she folded it, and only now, after four years of living in her apartment, only now did I see that she slightly resembled Mrs Wietzel, only slightly, but she did. Now, too, I saw for the first time how old she was: forty at least, maybe more. She had a cigarette in her mouth and was now shaking her apron, listening for matches in the pocket; there weren't any, and I also slapped my pockets in vain, I had left mine in my room, so I handed her my burning cigarette, she held it against hers, inhaled deeply, and handed it back to me: she smokes as I have seen only men smoke: yearningly, naturally, inhaling deep into her lungs.

"What a day!" she said. "In the end I stopped taking messages, it seemed pointless since you'd disappeared. Why did you forget that poor woman on Kurbel Street?"

I shrugged my shoulders and looked into her grey, slightly slanting eyes.

"Did you remember the flowers?"

"No," I said, "I forgot them."

119

She said nothing, in her embarrassment fiddled with the cigarette in her hand, leaned against the wall, and I knew she was finding it hard to say what she wanted to say. I wanted to help her, but couldn't find the words; she wiped her forehead with her left hand, saying: "Your supper's in the kitchen." But my supper was always in the kitchen, and I said, "Thank you," and looked past her and said quietly into the wallpaper pattern: "Say it."

"It's not like me," she said, "it's not pleasant for me, and it's painful for me to have to tell you I'd rather you didn't—I'd rather the girl didn't spend the night with you."

"Did you see her?" I asked.

"No," she said, "but I heard you both; it was so quiet—well, and suddenly I knew. Is she going to stay with you?"

"Yes," I said, "she's—she's my wife."

"Where did you get married?" She wasn't smiling, and I stared at the wallpaper pattern: at the orange triangles. I said nothing.

"Look," she said softly, "you know I hate saying it, but I can't stand things like that. I can't, and I have to tell you, not only tell you: it's impossible, I . . ."

"There are such things as emergency marriages," I said, "like there are emergency baptisms."

"Come on," she said, "don't give me that. We're not in the desert here, and we're not in the wilderness where there are no priests."

"We two," I said, "we two are in the desert and we are in the wilderness, and wherever I look I can't see a priest who would marry us." And I closed my eyes as they were still smarting from the scourging the headlights, and I was tired, dead tired, and could feel the pain in my hands. The orange triangles were dancing before my eyes.

"Or do you know of one?" I asked.

"No," said Mrs Brotig, "I don't."

I picked up the ashtray from the chair by the phone, stubbed out my cigarette, and held the ashtray out to her; she flicked the ash off her cigarette into it and took the ashtray from me.

I had never been so tired in all my life. My eyes were continually being pierced by the orange triangles as if by thorns, and I hated her husband for buying such things because they are what he calls "modern". "You might think of your father. You love him, don't you?"

"Yes," I said, "I love him, and I've thought of him many times today"—and I thought of Father again, saw him writing in blood-red ink on a big square sheet of paper: "Have a talk with the boy."

I first became aware of Hedwig in my landlady's eyes: a dark line in that kindly grey. I didn't turn around, I felt her hand on my shoulder, her breath, and I could smell that she had put on some lipstick: a waxy sweetness.

"This is Mrs Brotig," I said, "and this is Hedwig."

Hedwig held out her hand to Mrs Brotig, and I saw how large Hedwig's hands are, how white and how strong, when Mrs Brotig's hand lay in hers.

We were all silent, and I could hear a tap dripping in the kitchen, could hear a man's footsteps on the street, could tell from his footsteps that he had just knocked off work, and I was still smiling, smiling without knowing how, for I was really too tired to make that tiny movement of the lips which goes to make a smile.

Mrs Brotig replaced the ashtray on the chair by the phone, threw her apron down beside it, the cigarette ash flew up, some particles settled like powder onto the dark-blue carpet. She lit a fresh cigarette from the old one and said: "Sometimes I forget how young you are, but now you must go, don't make me throw you out—now go."

I turned, drawing Hedwig by the arm behind me into my room; I groped in the dark for my car key, found it on the desk, and we walked down the stairs again in our muddy shoes. I was glad I hadn't put the car in the garage but had left it out on the street. My left hand had stiffened up and was a bit swollen, and the right one was very painful from the blow against the marble edge of the café table. I was tired and hungry, and I drove slowly back into town. Hedwig was silent, she held her pocket mirror up to her face, and I saw she was looking just at the reflection of her mouth; she took her lipstick out of her purse and drew it across her lips with a slow, firm sweep.

The Nudelbreite was still closed to traffic, and it was not yet eight as I drove past the church again and into Netzmacher Lane, along Korbmacher Lane, and stopped at the vacant lot outside the bakery.

The light was still on in Hedwig's room; I drove on, saw the maroon car still parked outside the door, and drove right around the block back to the vacant lot in Korbmacher Lane. It was quiet and dark; we were silent. My hunger came, passed again, came and went again, running through me like the shock waves of an earthquake. I suddenly remembered that the cheque I had sent Wickweber was no longer covered, and it occurred to me that Hedwig had never even asked me what I did for a living. The pain in my hands was getting worse, and when I closed my tormented eyes for a second I found myself dancing through eternities of orange triangles.

The light in Hedwig's room would go out this Monday that still had four hours left; the sound of the maroon car's motor would die in the distance— already I seemed to hear the motor burrowing into the night, leaving silence and darkness behind. There would be stairs to be walked up, doors to be softly opened and closed. Once again Hedwig studied her lips, once again drew her lipstick across them with a slow, firm sweep, as if they weren't red enough yet, and already I knew what I was only to know later.

Never before had I known that I was immortal and yet how mortal I was: I could hear the infants screaming as they were being murdered in Bethlehem, and their screams mingled with Alois Fruklahr's dying scream, a scream no one had heard but which now reached my ear; I could smell the breath of the lions that had torn the martyrs to pieces, could feel their claws like thorns in my flesh; I could taste the brine of the sea, bitter drops from the deepest depths, and I could look into pictures that spread beyond their frames like water overflowing its banks—landscapes I had never seen, faces I had never known, and I fell through these pictures

123

towards Hedwig's face, landing on Brolaski, on Helene Frenkel, on Fruklahr, falling through these faces again onto Hedwig, and I knew that her face was imperishable, that I would see her again, with a cloth over her face that she would suddenly tear away to reveal her face to Grömmig. Hedwig's face, that was invisible to my eyes because the night was so dark, but I no longer needed eyes to see her.

Pictures floated up out of the darkroom: I saw myself as a stranger bending over Hedwig, and I was jealous of myself; I saw the man who had accosted her, his yellow teeth, his briefcase, saw Mozart smiling at Miss Klintick, the piano teacher who used to live next door to us, and the woman from Kurbel Street was weeping into all these pictures, and still it was Monday, and I knew I didn't want to get ahead; I wanted to get back—where, I didn't know, but back.

Keel, Achill Island,
July–September 1955

28

Due 7 Days From Latest Date

JUN 6 1977	AUG 1 8 1977	DEC 1 2 1977	10
JUN 9 1977	AUG 2 7 1977	DEC 2 3 1977	JUL 2 8 1987
JUN 1 7 1977	SEP 2 1977	JAN 4 1978	
JUN 2 5 1977	SEP 1 7 1977	JAN 1 1 1978	
JUN 2 8 1977	SEP 2 7 1977	JAN 1 6 1978	
JUL 1 1977	OCT 1 8 1977	JAN 2 7 1978	
JUL 1 4 1977	OCT 2 2 1977	FEB 1 6 1978	WITHDRAWN
JUL 2 2 1977	NOV 9 1977	MAR 1 8 1978	
JUL 3 0 1977	NOV 3 0 1977	APR 2 9 1978	